ENDORSED

MARNI MANN

For Kimmi Street and Crystal Radaker—my sisters, my squad, my tribe.
I love you girls more than anything.

PROLOGUE

"FOR THE FIFTH overall pick in this year's NFL draft, the Tennessee Titans choose Shawn Cole, tight end from Florida State," the NFL commissioner announced as he stood on the stage.

Once my client's name was called, I got up from my chair and cheered as loud as Shawn's family. "That's our boy," I said, gripping the shoulders of Shawn's dad and shaking them.

All that fucking work had paid off.

It wasn't just the hours I'd logged from trying to convince Shawn that I was the best agent for him, something I'd pushed since the last day of his college football season, but it was also the months of negotiation it had taken to get him an NFL contract.

It was all worth it.

Shawn, smiling like the richest motherfucker, stood and hugged his mother first. He then moved to his three older sisters. The fourth and youngest sister, Samantha—a girl I'd been secretly fooling around with since I met her three days ago—he hugged next. And then, finally, he embraced his dad.

I was sitting the farthest away, and he reached me last.

1

He shook my hand and patted my arm as he hugged me. "We did it, man."

"You did it." I pulled back. "Now, go show the world why you deserve to be a Titan."

Shawn followed my order, climbing the steps and walking onto the stage. A Titans hat was immediately placed on his head, and a jersey with his name and number was handed to him. He held the jersey in front of him, his smile growing even larger as he turned it, so the audience could see both sides.

The cheering erupted.

I took a quick peek at Samantha. She had her hand over her mouth; those gorgeous, dark eyes were wide and emotional as she stared at her brother.

I'd told his family that Shawn would get drafted in the top twenty.

But fifth?

I couldn't fucking believe it.

Besides a few small endorsement deals and a soccer contract, this was my first big break. One that would get my name printed on every sports page across America. One that would prove to my boss that, even though I'd just recently graduated from college, I would continue working my ass off until I was the top sports agent in LA.

As I glanced back at Shawn, where he was now posing in front of the camera, my phone vibrated from inside my suit. I pulled it out, the screen lighting up with texts from Max and Brett and Scarlett—my best friends, who all worked at the same agency as me. Their messages congratulated me on the Titans contract and said we'd celebrate tomorrow when I got back to California. Before putting my cell away, an email came through. It was from the Titans, and it outlined Shawn's schedule and what was required of him in the next few days.

I reviewed it all and slipped the phone into my pocket,

waiting for Shawn to reach our aisle before I said, "Are you ready to get back to work?"

"Hell yeah."

"The Titans want you to report to their training facility tomorrow afternoon. That means, instead of flying home to Florida, you'll be heading to Nashville."

"I'm down for whatever they want."

"Good," I said, pounding his fist. "Then, tonight, we celebrate."

"Tonight, we're getting fucking drunk," he promised.

And, hell, he kept that goddamn promise.

By one that morning, Samantha and I wanted to slip out of the bar and go back to our hotel for some alone time. We'd partied enough. So, she mentioned to her family that she was ready to go to bed, and I told Shawn I would escort her to the hotel.

I hadn't been able to keep my fucking hands off her, and after three days of foreplay, I was ready for more.

She was the most beautiful girl I'd ever seen. She didn't just deserve my attention; her presence demanded it.

And she had all of it—my hands and my mouth whenever one of her family members wasn't looking, my stare even if they were.

And, now, we were going to be by ourselves, and we wouldn't have to hide what we were doing.

I held her hand while we caught a taxi outside the bar in lower Manhattan, and we were driven to Midtown. We stumbled out of the back seat, and as I walked her into the lobby, my arm snaked around her waist.

"Shawn is going to be *sooo* far away now," she slurred.

I wasn't paying attention to her words. I was too focused on her body. As I held it tightly against my side, I was so turned on. Her heat, her smell, her touch—I wanted more, and I wanted it now.

"Nashville isn't even close to Florida, and I'm all the way down in Miami," she continued. "How will I see his games?"

"Your brother will be making enough that he can fly you there every weekend."

"You think?"

As we reached the elevator, I hit the button to take us upstairs. "I know."

"But he could get cut, couldn't he? And then what would happen?"

I turned her toward me. Those thick, glossy lips were begging me to kiss them. "Then, I'd find him a new team. But that's not going to happen. He's too good."

"You're so sure."

I put my hand on the back of her head, tilting her face up to mine. "Tennessee just lost one of their starting tight ends. They need someone with your brother's height and speed and with hands as quick as his. As long as he doesn't get injured during camp, he's got the starting spot."

"You're so sexy when you talk football."

I gripped her harder, my mouth moving closer to hers until I heard the elevator open. Then, my hand dropped to her waist again, and I led her inside, hitting the button for my floor. My room was where she'd chosen to hang out tonight.

"Make it move faster," she said, referring to the speed in which we were climbing.

She wrapped her hands around my arm, and she licked across her top lip. I couldn't pull my fucking eyes away.

It was so hard to make sure her brother had been occupied each time I kissed her. But at six-six, Shawn had three inches and a good thirty pounds on me. He was my top client. I sure as fuck didn't want him to see me all over his nineteen-year-old sister, who lived on the opposite side of the country as me, attending school at the University of Miami.

I didn't have to worry about that anymore.

"You think you have another drink in you?"

She hiccuped. "I know I do." I laughed, and she grabbed the lapels of my suit. "I majored in partying last semester. You know, all freshmen do their first year in college."

"I remember. I was one once."

The door slid open, and I brought her to my room. Once we were inside, she went to the minibar and scanned the shelves. She pulled out four small bottles of vodka and held them in the air.

"These will do," she said, handing me two and then climbing on top of the bed, gently bouncing while she guzzled the first one. Once the small bottle was empty, she dropped it onto the mattress and opened the second one. Right before it reached her mouth, she jumped, and the vodka splashed out. Some landed on her face and the rest on her shirt.

"Oh my God," she screeched, using her sleeve to wipe it off her skin.

I set both of my bottles on the dresser—one full, the other in my stomach. I'd taken it down like a shot as I watched her jump, her fucking nipples hardening more with each bounce.

"I'll get you a towel."

I went into the bathroom, grabbing the hand towel by the sink, and I returned to the bed.

Samantha was sitting on the mattress with her shirt off, holding it up in the air for me to see. "It's soaked."

The only thing I was focused on was her tits. They were held tightly in a black strapless bra, her pink nipples poking through the lace.

Jesus, fuck.

She had curves. She had the smoothest-looking skin. She had the kind of body I wanted to worship, that I wanted to taste until my tongue was too tired to lick anymore.

5

"Do you want a T-shirt to put on?"

She shook her head, and I took several steps closer until I stood in front of her. Using my knee, I slid her legs apart and moved in between them.

I wanted her bra off.

I wanted her jeans on my goddamn floor.

I wanted her lips around the end of my cock.

She was Shawn's sister, and I was playing with fucking fire.

"You have way too much on." Her hands went to my belt, and she unhooked it, unbuttoning and unzipping my suit pants. As they fell to the floor, she started on my jacket and shirt, and suddenly, I had on only a T-shirt and my boxer briefs.

I ran my fingers across her cheek, the look in her eyes telling me she was waiting for me to make the next move. My thumb then dipped lower and found a slick spot on her chin, a place she must have missed where the vodka had spilled. I brought my thumb up to my mouth and licked it off.

"Your brother can never know what happens in here. If he ever found out, it could ruin my career."

"I know." She blushed. "I'm going to go wash my face."

I stopped myself from putting my hand back on her. "Go do that."

She slid to the side and slowly rose from the bed.

"Fuck," I groaned as I watched her take a step, her smile pulling me in as much as her tits. "Your body is incredible."

She stood next to me, and I turned toward her. She ran her hands up her sides until they landed on her tits, two fingers brushing over her nipples.

The liquor had made her more confident.

I liked this version, and I liked how innocent she had acted before she started drinking.

But this sexual side was hot as hell, and it was fucking

dangerous. My cock didn't seem to care; the goddamn thing was so hard, the tip was grinding against my stomach.

"Go wash your face, and come right back," I told her.

Once I heard the bathroom door close, I took off my T-shirt and flopped down onto the bed. I pulled the blanket back, got my feet under it, and tucked the rest of it over me, my head sinking into the pillow.

My contract with Shawn was for three years. I couldn't have him find out what happened in this room, and I couldn't have him pissed off at me. I was just starting my career. This wasn't a good way to kick it off.

But, damn, that girl was seductive as fuck.

And I wanted her.

And I'd have her the second she returned to this bed.

I'd taste. I'd eat. I'd kiss every inch of that skin until she was screaming so loud, the only thing left to give her was my cock.

As I waited for her, I thought about how her pussy would feel.

How warm it would be.

How tight it would clench my dick.

And, just as I imagined what she would look like naked, I heard the sound of the bathroom door. My eyes shot to the entryway as I waited for her to step out. It took her a few seconds to round the corner. When she did, I saw that she'd taken her jeans off, and she was standing in front of me in just her strapless bra and a pair of matching panties.

"Get over here," I ordered.

She stopped when she reached the foot of the bed. "What are you going to do to me, handsome?"

"I'm going to fucking devour you."

She shook her head, a smile growing over that gorgeous face. "You're a naughty man, Jack Hunt."

"Naughty doesn't happen until I rip off those panties and put my tongue on your pussy."

With my head pounding from how much I'd drunk last night, I gently opened my eyes and slid out from underneath Samantha's arms, getting up to search for my ringing phone. I found it in my jacket and turned off the alarm I'd set.

It was a little past six, which meant my flight was in three hours.

Knowing I needed food more than a shower, I put my feet through the leg holes of my boxer briefs. Once those were on, my pants were next, followed by all the other clothes I'd dropped on the floor last night.

I went into the bathroom to do a quick brush of my teeth before tossing all my shit into my suitcase, which I rolled to the door.

Samantha hadn't moved in the bed. Her hair was fanned across the white pillow, the blanket pulled up to her neck. I leaned down and pressed my lips against her forehead.

"Good-bye, gorgeous girl," I whispered into her cheek.

She didn't even stir.

I went to the door, taking one last look behind me, and then I closed it, moving down the long hallway.

After a long cab ride, I checked in at the airport, and once I reached my gate, I reclined in one of the seats and took out my phone. It was late in LA, but I had a feeling Brett would still be up.

Me: Yo, you awake?
Brett: How was last night?

Me: The draft was sick. Fifth? That's some serious shit. I still can't believe it.

Brett: You worked hard for that one. Cha-ching.

Me: And I partied hard to celebrate. I'm hungover as fuck.

Brett: Are you going to make your flight?

Me: Yeah, I'm good. So, I met the girl of my fucking dreams.

Brett: And?

Me: Best sex I've ever had in my life.

Brett: Then, why don't you bump your flight a couple of days and spend some more time with her?

Me: I can't have her.

Brett: Why?

Me: She's Shawn Cole's little sister.

Brett: Fuck, man, you're right. Cut that shit off right now. Don't risk it. It's career-ending; you know that. Remember, clients first. Always.

Me: Mother. Fucker. I'll see you when I get home.

PROLOGUE

SAMANTHA - EIGHT YEARS AGO

AFTER I FINISHED WASHING the vodka off my face, I slipped out of my jeans and left them on the counter in the bathroom. I didn't need them on anymore. Not with the way things had been heating up before I spilled the booze all over me.

It had been three days of nonstop flirting and messing around with my brother's agent.

Three days of teasing.

I wanted this man, and tonight, I was going to have him.

I took a final peek at myself in the mirror, brushing away the fallen specks of eye shadow and fixing my eyeliner, and then I walked in the hallway and around the corner to the bedroom.

Jack was in bed, a blanket covering him from the waist down. He looked so incredibly hot. His chest was bare, extremely toned and defined. There was a delicious amount of scruff on his face, and he stared at me with a narrow gaze, those skilled, large hands resting over the comforter.

He wasn't a college student.

He wasn't a twenty-something dropout.

He was a businessman who had a real job, working with athletes and getting them signed to professional leagues.

Nothing was sexier than that.

Except for the way he was staring at me, like he wasn't going to leave this room until he feasted on every part of me.

And except for the suit he'd worn tonight. It was navy, and he'd paired it with a crisp white button-down, a striped tie, and brown leather shoes.

He didn't just act the part.

He dressed it, too.

"Get over here," he growled.

I got to the end of the bed and said, "What are you going to do to me, handsome?" I smiled, excited to hear his response.

"I'm going to fucking devour you."

I'd been wet since he started touching me at the bar. It was just casual then—a quick skim of his thumb across my cheek, a grasp of my thigh, a hold of my lower back. But, now, the anticipation of what he was going to do was making my body scream.

"You're a naughty man, Jack Hunt."

"Naughty doesn't happen until I rip off those panties and put my tongue on your pussy."

Oh God.

"Then, what are you waiting for?"

"Get on the bed."

It was an order. One that was full of lust and passion and dominance.

I pressed my hands onto the mattress, and my knees followed. I began to crawl, and when I reached the halfway point, he gripped me under my arms and flipped me onto my back, moving between my legs.

"Yes," I moaned.

He hadn't even really touched me yet.

"I want your fucking pussy." He tugged at the sides of my

lace panties until there was a hole, and then he shredded them off me, his mouth immediately covering my clit. "You taste so good." With one long stroke of his tongue, I heard, "Mmm, I can't get enough of it."

The back of my head ground into the pillow, my hands clenched the blanket, and I groaned. I couldn't believe how amazing this felt, that a man's tongue could feel as good as his dick.

Only one other guy's mouth had ever been in that spot. Whatever he had done was nothing like what Jack was doing right now.

Just when I thought it couldn't feel any better, he stuck a finger inside me.

I bucked from the sensation, the orgasm now within a few licks, and he was relentlessly swiping across my clit.

"More," I begged even though I had no idea what more would even feel like.

He filled me with another finger.

His flicking then turned faster, the orgasm pounding through me. My body quivered with each ripple that passed, and I heard myself shout after every wave.

He knew when I'd calmed because he pulled his mouth away, and he flipped me onto my stomach, quickly jumping off the bed for a few seconds before he moved in behind me, his face leaning into my neck. "Did that feel good?"

"Yes."

I heard the tearing of foil. "I can make you feel even better."

I moaned again, unsure of how that was even possible. "Your fingers. Your tongue." I shuddered. "If your dick is anything like them, I don't doubt it."

He laughed, and his whiskers scratched my cheek and shoulder, the skin so sensitive in those places that, "*Ahhh*," came hissing out of my mouth.

After roughing them up, he kissed both spots, and then he slowly traveled down my spine. "Patience. You're going to get what you want. But, right now, I'm still getting what I want." He continued to go lower until he reached my ass where he licked around the edge, skipping the middle to move to the other side. "Fucking perfect," he groaned, squeezing the bottom of my cheeks with his hands.

I gripped the feather pillow so hard.

Jack was so giving, so attuned to what I wanted, what I needed.

I'd never had anything like that before.

Nor had I had this kind of teasing, waiting for a surprise every time his mouth landed on my skin.

And it all felt so unbelievably good.

"Do you want me?" His voice vibrated across my skin.

That was the hottest question I'd ever been asked.

His lips were at the top of my ass, moving toward my side. "Yes."

In fact, I couldn't remember the last time I had wanted something this badly. My pussy was throbbing, there was pressure in my clit that needed to be released, and I couldn't get the thought of his hands and tongue out of my head.

"Then, tell me, Samantha."

He licked me again. This time, in the middle of my back, followed by a kiss and a quick swipe of his tongue.

"Oh God, Jack."

"Is your cunt nice and wet for me?"

I didn't even have to check. I could feel it on my inner thighs and on the blanket as it rubbed against me. "I'm dripping."

"Mmm, that's just what I want."

I barely had time to take a breath before his cock was at my entrance, and it was plunging straight inside me.

"*Ahhh*," I moaned so loudly.

ENDORSED

He was so large, so hard, and he moved with so much force and speed. After several thrusts, he slowed, pulling all the way out, pausing for several seconds before going back in.

I could feel the build coming on right away, especially as he twisted his hips when he was completely buried, reaching a spot no one had touched before.

That triggered a whole different kind of pleasure.

"Jack..."

"I fucking love it when you say my name."

"Harder," I demanded.

His face was in my neck, and I felt each breath he took, each groan, each nip he bit along my ear. "You're so tight, you're squeezing my tip every time I pull out." He held my hair in his hand and used it to lean my head back, giving him more access to my neck. "Do you want to come again?"

"Yes."

"Then, beg me."

My clit was grinding against the blanket. His cock was so deep inside me, there were sparks pulsing through my body. I was seconds away from losing it, and I swore, he could tell.

"I want to come," I cried. "Please, Jack. Oh God, please let me come."

"Those are the words I wanted to hear." His speed doubled, and so did his strength. His hips twisted in a circle as he got to the base, thrusting right back in when he reached his crown. "Your pussy is squeezing my cock, so I can feel how close you are." He put his mouth to the side of my face. "Fucking kiss me."

I turned my head, and I was immediately hit with his lips. His tongue touched mine, and the most sexual taste filled my mouth.

I didn't know how, but his power became more intense, now reaching the deepest part of me.

"Jack," I moaned.

15

This orgasm wasn't as quick and sharp as the first time he'd gotten me off.

This time, it was a slow, violent flare that didn't rush. It gradually dragged through my body, giving pleasure to each of my limbs before it sat in my navel and caused me to tremble.

"Fuck yes." He pulled his mouth away but stayed close, his teeth gnawing on my shoulder. "You're going to make me come."

I began to meet his strokes, my ass pushing back every time he slid forward, the orgasm still working its way through me.

"That's it, baby," he urged. "Just like that." I met him again and again until I heard him yell, "Samantha! Fuck!"

I loved how sexy he sounded as he came.

I loved how his strokes turned more aggressive.

And I loved how we both stilled at the same time.

Staying inside me, he kissed across my cheek until he reached my mouth where he moaned, "You're fucking incredible."

Me: Thanks for the most amazing three days and the most memorable trip to NYC. I just landed in Miami. Maybe I can come to LA in a few weeks to see you.

Jack: Hey, Samantha. It was a great couple of days for me, too, but it's time for us to return to our normal lives. I don't think LA is a good idea. Maybe I'll see you at one of your brother's games.

Me: Okay...is everything all right?

Me: If you're worried I'll say something to my brother, don't be. I wouldn't ever say anything. I just...miss you. That's why I've been texting so much.

Jack: Samantha, I know you promised never to discuss what happened that night in my hotel room, and I really appreciate that you haven't. You're a beautiful girl, and it's a few days I'll never forget. But, now that I've thought about our time together, I've realized it was a mistake. One that can never happen again. Your brother is my top client. I can't jeopardize that. Therefore, my relationship with his family has to stay professional. I'm sorry. Best of luck with your classes this semester. —Jack

Me: Jack, I need you to call me. I really need to talk to you.

Me: Jack, I've left you three voice mails. Please call me.

Me: I've left you six voice mails, three emails, countless texts. All I want is to talk to you.

Jack: I've gotten all of your messages. I've been extremely busy. Samantha, what happened between us has to stay in the past. I need you to stop contacting me and move on with your life. You can never be more than my client's little sister.
Me: Got it. Loud and clear. You won't ever hear from your client's little sister again.

1

JACK

"RUUUN!" I shouted at the TV.

I dropped my legs from the ottoman and moved to the edge of the couch while I watched Tennessee's running back make a fucking beeline for the end zone.

It was the divisional round playoffs, and they were up against San Diego, down by two touchdowns with nine minutes left in the fourth.

Tennessee's coach had been calling the wrong plays the whole game. I didn't know what the fuck was wrong with him. But, finally, he had called something the players could work with and they looked like they were gaining some momentum.

"That's it," I said to the TV. "Twenty more yards. You've got this."

My star tight end, Shawn Cole, had tweaked his hamstring a few days ago during practice, and he wasn't in tonight's game. Even though Tennessee's offense was strong without him, I could feel Shawn's absence, and I was sure San Diego could feel it, too.

"Ten more yards," Brett said from the other side of the couch. "He needs to run faster; they're right on his fucking tail."

I agreed.

I reached for my beer and held it to my lips, swallowing until it was gone.

"Jesus," Max said from the cushion next to mine. "It's about time their offense woke up."

The running back reached the end zone, and I put my beer down and clapped my goddamn hands together. "Down by one. Now, we need an interception."

Max took a bite of his pizza and said, "If San Diego scores on the next drive, it's going to take some aggressive offense to even this shit out, and Tennessee hasn't been playing aggressively at all."

"We've seen teams score with less than ten seconds left," Scarlett said, sitting between Brett and Max. "We have plenty of time to win this."

Brett, Max, and Scarlett, my best friends and business partners, were as invested in this game as I was. That was because, the further Tennessee advanced in the playoffs, the larger Shawn's bonus would be. As his agent, I would get a piece of that, and so would The Agency, the company the four of us had opened six years ago.

Even though I represented some of the top athletes in the world, Shawn was ranked one of the highest, and he'd never made it to the Super Bowl. He deserved the championship, and this year, he was so fucking close to playing in it.

"Tennessee's defense is finally stepping it up," Brett said after the first play. "We need to keep them from getting in field goal range."

"You think they'll go for three and not seven?" Max asked.

"They have one of the best kickers in the league," Brett replied.

Scarlett held open the pizza box and said, "Who needs a slice?"

Brett took one, but I shook my head. "I just need beer."

"I'm empty, too," Max said. "I'll grab us some." He walked over to the bar that I'd had built in my living room, opened the fridge, and handed me one.

I screwed off the cap and brought it up to my lips just as a flag was thrown. "What kind of fucking call was that?"

"Fifteen yard penalty and automatic first down," the ref said.

"I can't fucking watch this." I got up from the couch and moved into the kitchen, pacing around the goddamn island, hearing the TV but not turning toward it.

Had Miami not played this afternoon, I probably would have gone to Tennessee to see Shawn and to watch the game. But the Dolphins quarterback was looking for a new agent now that his contract with his current one was almost up. Agents from all over the country had been pitching him this week. And, after his game today, I had as well, bringing my partners with me so that he could meet the whole team and get a feel for us.

The Dolphins were having an after-party in South Beach tonight, and the quarterback had invited us to go. As a company, we had decided it was important for all of us to be there. That was the only reason I hadn't taken The Agency's private jet to Tennessee to watch the game. And, since Shawn was sitting this one out, I knew it was all right that I missed it.

"Third and six," Scarlett announced, like I couldn't fucking hear the TV.

If Tennessee lost to San Diego, Shawn would blame himself. He was so competitive, so dedicated; he gave everything to that team.

And, when he'd tweaked his hamstring, I knew it would cause him to have to sit this one out. Shawn didn't believe that. He thought he could fight through the pain and convince the team doctor to clear him for the game.

Minutes before the players had gone out on the field, Shawn

had called me to see if there was anything I could do to change the doctor's mind. He knew damn well he could injure himself even worse. I didn't care if he was willing to take that risk. I wasn't, and his coaches weren't either.

"Interception."

I stopped circling the kitchen and faced the living room. "What?"

"Interception," Max called out again. "Tennessee's ball."

"You're shitting me."

But I could tell he wasn't because the announcers were shouting, and the crowd was roaring. And, now, the commentators were explaining how it had happened, at what yard line, and who had caught the ball.

"You have to come in here and watch this," Brett said.

I circled around the rest of the island and moved into the living room. "We have a chance," I sighed, sitting in the same seat as before. "We finally have a fucking chance."

Scarlett laughed. "I'm pretty sure I already told you this."

Max looked at Scarlett and me and said, "There's still seven minutes left. Let's just hope they've found their rhythm."

"It only took them three and a half quarters," Brett mocked.

"Listen," Scarlett said, "they've found it, and that's all that matters right now."

"They need—"

I was cut off when Max stood from the couch and shouted at the tight end, "Run! Run that fucking ball!"

"Forty yards," I said, counting each white line he passed. "Thirty-seven."

"He's going to make it," Scarlett cheered.

"How are you so sure?" Brett asked her.

"Look at how fast he's going." She pointed at the screen. "There isn't a single person on that field who has that kind of speed."

There was a player gaining traction on our tight end, and it worried the hell out of me.

"He needs to watch out for number fifty-four," I said. "He's about to be right on his ass."

"Twenty yards," Max said.

"Trust me," Scarlett told us all, "he's got this."

"If Tennessee scores, I'm skipping the Dolphins party, and I'm taking Scarlett to the casino," Max said.

"You're not skipping the party," Scarlett snapped. "That's the whole reason we're not in Tennessee right now."

"Ten yards," I said.

"You know, I really should have bet the three of you that Tennessee would win this game. It would have made the next few minutes so much more interesting," Scarlett said.

"Touchdown," the announcer said.

I could finally take a goddamn breath.

But I only had time for one. There was still six and a half minutes left in the game. That gave San Diego plenty of time to take the lead again.

When the TV switched to a commercial, Scarlett asked Brett, "When is James flying back?"

James Ryne, an Oscar-winning actress and one of the coolest girls I knew, was Brett's fiancée. She was also his client—something that hadn't changed and wouldn't now that they were engaged. She split her time between Miami and wherever she was filming, and that meant Brett spent more time on the road, so he could see her.

"Tomorrow," Brett replied.

"And Eve?" Scarlett asked Max.

"Not sure," he said. "Not for at least a few more weeks."

Eve Kennedy was James's best friend, a celebrity stylist, and Max's girlfriend. She lived in LA and traveled all over the world for her clients. Max didn't see her as often as he'd like, and I knew that was becoming tough for him.

Scarlett and I didn't have to worry about any of that shit because we were both single.

Most of that was due to me working so damn much. It was almost impossible to date women outside my industry. None of them understood the time I dedicated to my clients or the schedule I had to maintain to make sure they were successful.

Unlike Brett, who ran our acting division, and Max, who managed the music department, I worked with mostly men. Therefore, I didn't have the luxury of being around beautiful women who were sympathetic because they put in as many hours as me. And no amount of time was ever enough for the ladies I'd been with in the past. So, I kept things casual, I focused on my athletes, and I built The Agency's sports division to the highest-grossing in the country.

For now, that was enough.

When the commercial break ended, the screen now showing the field again, the teams were getting in their positions for the kickoff. San Diego was on the receiving end and ran it to the thirty-yard line. Just as our defense was getting the play called, I felt my phone vibrate.

I yanked it out of my pocket and quickly checked the screen, seeing that it was the quarterback from Miami.

"Fuck," I hissed. "I have to take this call."

"Want me to pause the game?" Max asked.

I ground my teeth together. "No. Hopefully, this won't take too long."

I got up from the couch and went into my bedroom, connecting the call before it went to voice mail. "Jack Hunt here."

"I just heard Rolex is shopping for a new face. I want that

face to be mine. If you can get me that contract by tonight's party, then you'll be my agent."

I checked my watch and did the math in my head. It was almost four in the morning in Geneva where Rolex's headquarters was located.

"I need twenty-four hours," I told him.

"You have three. I'll see you at the party."

He hung up, and I stared at the home screen, thinking of whom I could call. Brett and Max had the same connections as me, and Scarlett was our CFO, so I was positive none of them would be able to help.

I needed someone with European contacts.

Someone who would pick up the goddamn phone.

And then it came to me.

I scrolled through my numbers until I found the one for Phillip.

He answered after the second ring. "Do you have any idea what time it is?" he said in a groggy British accent.

Geneva was one hour ahead of London, so I knew exactly what time it was there.

"Sorry, man. I know it's early, but I need your help."

"At this hour?"

"I have a potential client who wants the Rolex contract. Do you know anyone there?"

Phillip was the highest-earning sports agent in the UK. He had his own agency and represented athletes in Europe, Asia, and South Africa. When he needed a contact in the States, he called me.

It was time for him to return the favor.

"Aren't you just a lucky motherfucker, mate? I happen to know their head of marketing. We go on holiday together."

"I knew I was reaching out to the right guy. Can you set up a three-way call?"

"Right now?"

"Yes, Phillip, right now."

"Give me a second." I heard what sounded like him walking across a hard surface and then a slow flow of running water. When it shut off, he said, "I'm going to put you on hold while I try him."

I paced my bedroom and went as far as the bathroom, circling the side of the tub and passing the large walk-in shower, steam room, and both sets of sinks. By the time I made it to the entrance of my closet, I heard Phillip come back on the line.

"Jack?" Phillip said.

"I'm here."

"I have Elias Schmid on the phone. Elias is the head of marketing for Rolex and a dear friend of mine." He paused for a second. "Elias, like I briefly mentioned, Jack Hunt is the US version of me."

"Mr. Hunt," Elias said.

"Call me Jack, please," I said, and I stopped in the middle of my room. "I apologize for my timing. I know how early it is in Geneva, but I wouldn't have called if it wasn't a pressing matter. News has reached the States that you're looking to rebrand Rolex, and you think a new face will help you do that."

"You've heard correctly, Jack."

I wanted to know why a player had heard this bit of information before me. My team should have been all over this. If their connections hadn't alerted them, then they needed stronger fucking roots. And that was what I'd tell them during our meeting tomorrow.

"I have a potential client who's about to ink a deal with Breitling. In fact, the contract is in his hands as I speak, and he'll be signing with the watch company within the next hour. Before his signature is permanently on that contract, I wanted to see if you were interested in stealing him from Breitling."

"Who's the client?"

"Vince Hedman."

I heard him take in a deep breath. "As in the quarterback for the Miami Dolphins?"

"The same one."

"I'm glad you reached out." He paused. "Would Mr. Hedman be interested in a full international advertising campaign? Attending several industry events in the States and abroad? Being seen with only a Rolex during the entire commitment of his contract?"

Now that I was getting somewhere, I sat on the bench at the foot of my bed. "Vince is extremely particular about what jewelry he wears. Most of his pieces are custom-made. But, if you'd like him to wear your brand exclusively, I'm sure we could discuss that during contract negotiations."

"I need to speak to my team."

"Of course," I said.

"But, on behalf of Rolex, I would like to say that we're extremely interested in Mr. Hedman, and I would like him to hold off on signing with Breitling."

"Unfortunately, Elias, I can put things on hold for only so long. Vince's signature is due by midnight, Eastern Standard Time."

"Jack, please give me your number. I'll reach out to my team, and I'll phone you right back."

While I gave him what he'd asked for, I walked over to the doorway of my bedroom to try to hear the TV. The guys had turned it down, so I couldn't make out anything the commentators were saying.

"I'll be in touch," Elias said and hung up.

I stayed on the line and said to Phillip, "Are you still there?"

"You owe me, motherfucker."

"We'll call it even for the Ford and Nike contracts I helped you land."

"And the Gatorade contact you're going to give me once I get to the office."

I laughed. "We'll see about that. Thanks for your help, Phillip."

I disconnected the call, and as I walked out of my room, I kept my phone in my hand in case Elias called back.

"What's the score?" I asked, rounding the corner to the main living space.

The TV was showing a soda commercial.

"The game is over," Brett said.

"What was the fucking score?" I repeated.

The three of them looked at me, smiles slowly spreading across their faces.

"Shawn is going to the next round," Max said.

"*Fuuuck* yeah," I said as I joined them on the couch. "Shawn must be so goddamn happy right now."

In an hour, once things settled down in the locker room, I'd call him to congratulate him. First, he needed some time to celebrate with his team. Besides, I was positive all he'd want to talk about was his eligibility for the next game and to make sure he'd get the doctor's clearance.

"Everything all right with the call you got?" Brett asked.

I nodded. "It was Vince. He wants a deal with Rolex before he signs with me."

"And?" Scarlett said.

"I'm pretty sure I just got him one."

"Sounds like it was a good fucking day," Max announced, going over to the bar to grab everyone a beer.

"It's going to be even better when we go to the party and tell Vince the news." I took the beer Max handed to me and held it up in the air, waiting for the other three to join me. "Tonight, we're going to fucking celebrate."

"Cheers to that," they all said.

2

SAMANTHA

"WE WON, SAM," my brother, Shawn, said as I held the phone to my ear, my other hand gripping an extra-large coffee. "We fucking destroyed them."

I'd been listening to the game since I landed at LAX. The Titans had advanced and would be up against the Dolphins in the Super Bowl.

Every time one of the announcers had called my brother's name, the guilt of not being there grew even more. And hearing the moment they'd won was like a knife stabbing the back of my throat.

I should have been there.

But I was in the back seat of this giant SUV instead, being driven to a client's house—a client who'd had two dates available to meet with me, and I chose this one, knowing it was my brother's game.

"I told you, you were going to destroy them," I said. "And, now, you're going to the Super Bowl."

I'd only been waiting eight seasons to say that to him.

"Miami is a hell of a team."

"So is Tennessee." I sipped the coffee, hoping the caffeine would kick in soon. "Your team is healthy. More importantly, your hamstring is completely healed. You're going to go out on that field, play the sport you love, and prove once again why you're one of the best tight ends in the world."

"You're going to be there, right?"

I'd known that question was coming.

I'd known the second my phone rang.

I closed my eyes, pushing the back of my head into the seat, and exhaled. "Of course. I wouldn't miss it." I cringed as the words left my mouth.

I'd said the same exact thing during preseason when he asked if I would be at his first game, which I didn't end up attending. Then, I'd missed all of his home games but two and each round of the playoffs.

At least my parents and my three sisters had gone to all of his games.

It was only me who hadn't made it.

Only me who had taken a different path than the rest of my family.

The driver weaved down the narrow street and pulled up to a gate, stopping next to a call box. He pushed the button and said, "I have Samantha Laine for Miss Ryne."

A buzz came through the speaker, and the gate began to open.

"Shawn, I have to run. I just got to my client's house. But, listen, I couldn't be happier for you, and I couldn't be prouder. I hope you celebrate so hard tonight because you've certainly earned it."

"I'll see you in a few weeks."

I quickly shut my eyes again at the thought of that.

I took a deep breath.

I felt a gnawing pain in the pit of my stomach.

"You will. Now, go party."

I listened to him say good-bye, and then I slid the phone into my purse and put my hand through the loop of my computer bag, keeping the coffee close to my mouth.

Once the driver opened my door, I climbed out and walked up the front steps of the house. Before I had a chance to knock, the door opened.

"Samantha, I'm so happy you're here," James Ryne said, looking like she had just stepped off a movie set.

I'd been working with the Oscar winner for a while now, and I still had a hard time believing that I had a client as high profile as her.

Seeing how put together she was made me wish I'd touched up my makeup on the flight. I just didn't have the energy. Before driving myself to Miami International Airport, I'd overseen two installations and a buildout. It was a miracle I'd even gotten on the plane.

"Me, too," I said. "I'm excited to see your new house."

As I stepped inside the entrance, she gave me a hug. I squeezed her back, grateful that she liked my work enough to fly me all the way out here.

Once she released me, I glanced up at the twenty-foot ceiling, my mind immediately spinning with ideas for the foyer.

"I want this place to have a completely different feel than our home in Miami," she said. "Miami will be our permanent residence, so this will be more like our getaway and where I'll stay when I'm in town."

I took several steps forward and did a full turn, taking in the whole space. The walls were only primed, and the floors were cement. There wasn't even any material on the grand staircase.

"It's a blank canvas," I said, finally looking at her again.

It was more like a shell of drywall.

"I know I didn't mention that when we talked on the phone,

but I figured you'd prefer it that way to having to tear everything down."

"You're saying you want me to do the buildout as well?" I held my breath while I waited for her answer.

"Samantha, I want you to do it all—the construction, the design, the decorating. This is your baby."

Inside, I was screaming.

But, outside, I was really trying to play it cool.

The projects I'd completed for James weren't anything like this. I designed the most luxurious closet for her Miami penthouse. And, slowly, we added some feminine touches to the extremely masculine condo. That was because she had moved in with her fiancé, and we were trying to convert his bachelor pad into a space that suited the both of them.

But this was starting from the ground up.

This was where I could really show her my ideas.

This was a dream.

Out of all the interior designers in LA, she'd chosen me, who lived all the way in Miami.

I wouldn't let her down.

"Will you show me around?" I asked. "I want to get a feel for each room and take some pictures, so I can start working when I get back to Florida."

"Absolutely. Follow me."

I reached inside my computer bag and took out my camera, turning it on. I held it against my face, shooting several shots of the entrance. Once I had enough, I followed her to the first room on the right. I gasped when I saw it, its size and shape, the floor-to-ceiling windows that overlooked the backyard.

"Oh, James."

I felt her eyes on me. "Isn't it so perfect?"

I nodded. "This is going to make the most stunning kitchen."

I took photographs from each angle, knowing I'd also need

the blueprints because there were far too many measurements for me to take in one night.

"Tell me what you're feeling," she said. "Have any colors come to you yet? Textures? I know it's early, and you haven't seen much of the house, but I'm dying to know."

I walked to the middle of the room, envisioning the placement of the cabinets, a massive island, and an eat-in kitchen along the side.

"White with a touch of gray. Not a charcoal. I see a soft, sweet smoke." I moved to the wall on the right, running my fingers across the primer. "A carrara marble set in a basket weave for your backsplash. Each piece will be hand-cut, the lines going linear." I glanced up several inches. "White cabinets, shaker-style, with simple, clean hardware and ten-inch crown molding." I backed up, so I could take in the whole wall. "I want the countertops to be white stone with the same hint of gray."

"Classy and elegant."

Our eyes connected again.

"A place where you can come to relax."

She smiled.

"I'll use pops of color, but I want to pull those hues from out there." I pointed at the windows and moved toward them, overlooking the lit-up backyard. "Once we have the pool designed and installed and the landscaping done, I'll tie it all together. I want your outdoor and indoor living spaces to flow."

"I can't wait for Brett to hear this." Her smile grew even larger. "He's going to love everything you've said."

"A project like this has to be done in stages," I told her. "First, we'll plan and execute the interior and exterior buildout. Once it's finalized, we'll focus on the decorating. Construction this extensive will probably take four to six months. It's a process."

She leaned her side against the wall. "That's no problem. I have a rental since I've been doing so much filming here. And there's no rush. Besides, Brett and I are so busy; it's going to be hard to find time when we're both available to meet, and I want him involved with this."

I'd never met her fiancé. Anytime I had been at their home in Miami, he wasn't ever there. But I knew all about Brett and his partners since my brother was signed with their company. James and I never discussed that, and she would never make my connection with the famous Shawn Cole because, professionally, I went by my mother's maiden name.

I'd decided to do that the minute I graduated college.

I wanted my success to be my own. I wanted to earn it from hard work and dedication and skill. I never wanted Shawn to open any doors for me, and I never wanted them to open because of who he was.

Shawn knew how I felt, and he respected that.

"After I take a look at the blueprints, I'll put some designs together. We'll work around both of your schedules. I can make myself available day or night."

"You're wonderful, Samantha, and I'm certain you're the right person for this job."

I returned the smile, still trying to keep it cool. "I can't wait to start working on this project."

She looped her arm through mine. "Come on, there are twenty-two other rooms I need to show you along with the most incredible wine cellar you've ever seen."

3

JACK

AS SHAWN SAT on a chair in the locker room, dressed in everything but his jersey and helmet, I knelt in front of him and said, "Are you ready to go out there and fucking demolish the Dolphins?"

He ground his hands together, straightening his fingers and then tightening them into a fist. "Yes."

"Do you feel healthy?"

He stared straight ahead, never making eye contact, with his lips spread apart and his teeth bared. "Yes."

"Do you feel prepared?"

"Yes."

"Then, are you going to go out there and win yourself a goddamn Super Bowl?"

His fist punched the palm of his other hand. "Fuck yes."

That was the answer I wanted.

I patted him on the shoulder. "Get your jersey and your helmet on. Then, get your ass on that field, and go bring home a championship."

He finally glanced at me, the look in his eyes showing how ready he was. "You've got it."

I pounded his chest with the back of my hand, waiting for the glare to fade, for the intensity to break just a little.

It never did.

Nothing I could say would crack his concentration, so I knew he really was ready, and it was time for me to leave.

"Demolish them," I repeated.

With his jaw clenched, his eyes still so fucking fierce, I walked out and went upstairs to the VIP lounge where my partners were hanging out.

"How's he doing?" Max asked as I joined them at their table.

I responded, "Whom are you asking about? Vince or Shawn?"

The three of them laughed.

"Well, whom did you just meet with?" Scarlett asked. "Or did you visit both?"

"I started with Shawn," I said. "It felt wrong to go from one right to the other, so I'll visit with Vince in a little bit."

"Two clients on opposing teams, both playing in the Super Bowl. Now, isn't that some shit?" Brett said.

This wasn't the first time that had happened. The same scenario had occurred one year during the NBA championship and also the World Series.

In cases like this, I had to stay neutral, especially at the game. The last fucking thing I needed was a cameraman to catch me rooting for one team over another and pissing off one of my clients.

But, deep down, I always had a favorite.

And, since Vince already had a ring, I really wanted to see Shawn take this win.

"I assume Shawn's family is here?" Max asked.

I nodded, resting my elbows on the high-top table. "There's so many of them, they rented a box."

"Do you plan on going to see them?"

I checked my watch. The players didn't have to hit the field for another forty-five minutes. That gave me plenty of time to go talk to Shawn's family and then head to Vince's locker room.

"Yeah, and I'm thinking I should go now," I said.

"I'll go with you," Brett responded. "I'd like to congratulate them."

"I think we all would," Scarlett said.

Max nodded.

I stepped back from the table. "Follow me."

I led them through the lounge and out a back hallway where we took the elevator to the suite level of the stadium. After showing our passes to the security officers, we walked halfway around the building until we reached their suite.

I knocked on the door, and I extended my hand when Shawn's father's was the one to open it. "Mr. Cole."

"Jack, welcome. Come on in."

I waited for him to release me before I pointed behind me. "I brought my business partners. They'd like to meet you and your family."

"The more, the merrier."

I introduced him to Scarlett, Max, and Brett, and then we made our way inside the suite. I was surprised as hell to see how many people were in here. Yesterday morning, Shawn had told me there would be at least twenty, but I was sure there had to be over thirty. A good percentage was family members I'd met over the years at Shawn's games.

But the one face I looked for and couldn't find was Samantha's.

I hadn't seen her since the morning after the NFL draft when I kissed her forehead and left for my flight. If she'd attended any of Shawn's games, they weren't the ones I had been at.

I'd thought about her several times after I returned to LA and cut things off between us. But I never asked Shawn about her, he never brought her up, and I never searched for her online.

My client's sister was off-fucking-limits.

Ending things between us was the best thing for the both of us.

"Jack, have you spoken to our boy?" Shawn's father asked.

The room quieted, and I felt lots of eyes on me.

"I just saw him a few minutes ago," I said. "He's feeling prepared, and he's ready to go."

"How's his hamstring?" one of his sisters asked.

"Fully healed," I answered, feeling confident in my answer after an extensive conversion with the team doctor this morning. "Don't be concerned. He's healthy."

"And the rest of the team? Are they ready?" his mother asked.

"I watched their walk-through yesterday," I said. "The team looked strong and focused. They're ready—all of them."

"I hope we'll be seeing you at the after-party," another one of his sisters said.

"Wouldn't miss it," I responded, feeling like it was a good time to make our exit. I stepped toward Shawn's father and shook his hand again. "I'll see you after the game."

"Hopefully, it's down on the field," he said.

I smiled, giving a quick hug to Shawn's mother, and moved to the door. I knew the guys and Scarlett were right behind me, so I twisted the handle and went out into the hallway.

That was when I saw *her* approaching the suite.

When my stare traveled up that perfect fucking body and eventually stopped on her gorgeous face.

When my mouth opened, remembering the way hers had tasted.

When not a single goddamn word came out of me because I was far too busy taking her in.

4

SAMANTHA

AS I HUNG up with my client, I walked out of the back stairwell and made my way down the hallway. I'd escaped there for some privacy since it was far too loud in the suite to hear anything she was saying. With the phone still in my hand, I quickly checked my email, making sure nothing had come in that needed my immediate attention.

Knowing I was just a few suites away from the one we rented, I slipped my cell into my back pocket and looked up.

My feet stopped moving.

There was no way I could take another step.

Not with Jack Hunt standing in front of me, his eyes so locked with mine that I couldn't breathe.

He had come into my life eight years ago, uprooted every emotion I'd ever had, violently shaken them, and then stomped on them like they were bugs scurrying around his feet.

"Samantha."

It was a little louder than a whisper.

But it was enough to make my heart clench.

Because I'd thought about him every day since he left me in New York.

Because I'd cared about him.

Because he had owned my body for far too long.

"Jack," I gasped. "Hi."

Oh God, he was handsome. Even more so than he had been all those years ago.

He was older—we both were—but he'd aged so perfectly. He had crinkles around his eyes and deeper ones beside his lips. I remembered running my fingers through the scruff on his cheeks, which was now a full beard, and how it had roughed up my lips. His smile was sharp, piercing, and it still had the ability to make me wet. But what stood out the most were his eyes. They were a deep blue, the color of the sky right before it turned to dusk, a color I still saw every day.

"I was hoping you'd be here."

Hoping I'd be here?

Part of me wanted to laugh.

Part of me wanted to slap him.

And part of me wanted to wrap my fingers around the lapels of his suit jacket and scream, *Why?*

But I didn't say a word as he was joined by three other people —a woman and two men. One of the guys I knew was Brett Young, James Ryne's fiancé.

I should introduce myself to him. He was my client after all.

But I couldn't imagine opening my mouth. I certainly couldn't imagine trying to make any sense of the thoughts in my head.

"I'll meet you at the suite," Jack said to the others as he stayed standing by the door, blocking it so that I'd have to move past him to enter.

As the three of them went by, I felt their gaze.

I didn't look in their direction. I didn't say anything. I just focused on Jack, on that sexy face that had visited so many of my dreams, and I tried to keep it together.

"Samantha, you look amazing. How've you been?"

There were so many things I wanted to voice, and none would answer his question.

The safest thing to say was, "I'm good."

The grin on his lips was small, but it was growing.

I hated it.

And I loved it.

And I hated that I loved it.

"I've never seen you at any of his games."

He'd noticed.

That was interesting.

I wasn't nineteen anymore. I'd grown a backbone.

"After the last text you sent me, I'm surprised you've been looking for me."

I didn't glance away from the blue of his eyes.

It was holding me.

It was keeping me captive.

It was making me feel, and that was the last thing I needed right now.

He peered off to the side, rubbing his hand over his long whiskers. "I wish things had been different; you know that." He took a breath. "Will you be at the after-party?"

I wrapped my arms around my waist and thought of every reason I shouldn't be there. I thought of the excuses I could come up with. But every one of them would hurt Shawn. I'd missed so much, so much because of Jack. Whether Shawn won or lost, I had to be there.

"Yes."

He took several steps closer, and when he was less than a foot away, I watched his hand lift from his side and land on my shoulder. "Then, I'll see you later."

The things those fingers could do.

The way they could make me moan.

I had craved them so much.

I still did.

I didn't say a word as he moved another pace. I just continued to watch him until he got past me, and then I forced myself forward, clasping the doorknob and shoving myself inside the suite.

"Everything all right with work?" my mom asked once I closed the door and pressed my back against it.

I hadn't seen her standing there.

I hadn't taken a breath.

But, with him gone, now that I could breathe in a space that he wasn't in, I sucked in enough air to fill my lungs and looked at my mom.

"Honey?"

Several seconds passed before I said, "Sorry. What did you ask?"

She put her hand on my cheek, as though she was checking my temperature. "You look like you just saw a ghost."

Jack was someone my brother spoke about on occasion, someone I knew was a huge part of his life, someone he saw often.

But, to me, he was a ghost.

And it certainly felt like I had just seen one.

"I—"

"Auntie Sam," my three-year-old niece said, cutting me off, as she ran up to us, saving me from answering my mom's question. She hugged her tiny arms around my thigh. There were smudges of frosting on her cheeks that would soon be on my jeans if I didn't get a napkin and wipe it off. "Come up front with me." She tugged like she could move me. "We want you to sit with us."

I grabbed a napkin from a nearby table, and even though she

fought me on it, I was able to rub it across her cheeks. "You're all clean. Now, we can go sit."

She gave me the biggest smile as I carried her to the front of the suite. "Uncle Shawn's gonna win the football."

I laughed. "Uncle Shawn's definitely going to win the football tonight."

But that meant the party would be happening soon after the game. The one Jack would be at.

And, just like what had happened outside in the hallway, my entire world would be rocked.

This time, I'd be expecting it.

This time, I'd have a few glasses of wine in me.

And maybe, this time, I'd be able to respond without my entire body wanting to scream.

5

JACK

"TO THE BEST team in the NFL," Shawn toasted as he stood on a chair in the middle of the bar, holding a glass of beer in his hand.

"Hear, hear!" over three hundred partiers shouted back.

"To the best goddamn teammates I could ever have," he continued.

"Hear, hear."

"To the most loyal fans, the most supportive families, and one hell of a coaching staff," he added.

"Hear, hear."

"And to us"—he looked at all his teammates—"we kicked ass this season, we overcame every obstacle that was thrown our way, and we fought hard to be Super Bowl champions. Now, it's time to fucking party."

"Hear, fucking, hear."

He jumped off the chair, and I clinked glasses with him.

"My email is already blowing up with contracts," I told him. "So, you and your boys go celebrate. I'll give you tomorrow off to recover. But, come Tuesday morning, I'm flying to Nashville, and we've got some business to discuss."

"You're going to get me endorsed?"

I laughed, matching the expression on his face. "You're already endorsed. What I'm going to do is make you even richer than you already are."

He pounded his fist on my shoulder and said, "The best thing I ever did was sign with you. Eight seasons, and it's been one hell of a ride."

I held my glass up to my lips. "The ride is just starting, my man. You've got plenty more Super Bowls in you."

"You've got that right."

My fingers slapped and gripped his, and we went in for a man hug. "Go have fun. I'll see you later."

He released my hand, and I turned toward my partners, who were standing right behind us.

"What a fucking awesome night for The Agency."

"How much are we looking at?" Brett asked.

I quickly calculated the amounts sitting in my email, knowing which contracts Shawn would accept and which ones wouldn't be enough, and then I added up my percentage. "Our take will be close to five million. That's just from today. Tomorrow will bring in another impressive round, I'm sure."

"Damn," Max said. "You killed this month's numbers."

I smiled, looking at the amber liquor in my glass. "I didn't kill them. I fucking slaughtered them."

"He's showing us up," Brett said to Max.

"Do I smell a competition brewing?" Scarlett asked. "Because nothing makes me happier."

As our CFO, Scarlett was all about our numbers, and the three of us were so competitive that it fueled us if one did better than the other. Her suggestion only goaded us.

"Whoever has the highest month wins thirty grand from each agent. That's sixty total. Deal?" I said.

Brett stuck out his hand. "It's on, brother."

We clasped fingers, and then I did the same with Max.

Once we all agreed on the bet, a waiter stopped by and delivered another round of drinks.

As I was lifting the glass off the table, Max said, "I meant to ask you this when we were in our suite, but I got distracted by the game and forgot. Who was that girl outside the Coles' box?"

I held the scotch underneath my nose and briefly inhaled it, feeling the way it slightly burned my skin. "That was Samantha, Shawn's youngest sister."

He shook his head. "She's hot as hell."

Samantha Cole wasn't fucking hot.

She was gorgeous.

She was breathtaking.

She was perfect in every goddamn way.

And, if she weren't Shawn's sister, she'd be standing next to me at this table instead of on the other side of the bar, sipping a glass of wine while she spoke to Shelby, the oldest of the four girls.

I'd seen Samantha the second I arrived at the after-party. The sight of her reminded my cock of how fucking good her pussy had felt and how badly I had wanted her that night.

My need to be inside her hadn't changed.

If anything, it intensified, especially with how beautiful she looked and how well she knew how to fuck.

All I wanted right now was to move in behind her, spread her arms over the bar top, and pound her pussy from behind.

But the girl had barely glanced at me, our eyes only connecting once, and she hadn't done it since.

"It's about time she showed up," Brett said.

Brett was the only one in the group who knew about our past.

I'd never told any of the others, even after I ended things with her. It wasn't that I didn't trust them. I trusted Max and Scarlett with my life. There was just nothing to discuss; it was over before anything started.

But, man, she hadn't been easy to ignore.

Not when she called a few times, when she texted even more.

Once I'd sent her the message that severed things permanently, she replied, and then I never heard from her again.

"Showed up?" Scarlett said. "What does Brett mean by that?"

I leaned into the table, stealing a glance at Samantha before I looked at Scarlett. "I've never seen her at any of Shawn's games. That's what Brett means."

Scarlett nodded toward the right side of the room. "Isn't that her?"

I let out a painful sigh. "Yes."

When it came to business, I always got what I wanted. I was cutthroat, and I attacked like a goddamn lion. In my personal life, I wasn't as vicious. Women were gentle; they couldn't handle that kind of ruthlessness. Plus, I didn't have the time to hunt. I just went after what was available, and then I moved on.

With Samantha, I'd gone after her. I fucked her. And then I was forced to say good-bye. Halting things between us had fucking sucked.

And it sucked even harder, seeing how beautiful she was now, maybe even more so than when I'd first met her.

Samantha had an exoticness to her with bright olive skin and the biggest brown eyes. Her jeans were so tight, I could see the muscles in her thighs, the slight dip of her hips, and the roundness of her tight ass. I knew how fucking delicious every one of those spots tasted. But it was her face I couldn't get enough of. Those plump lips that she loved to lick and those cheeks that had reddened when my beard scratched them.

I felt Scarlett's eyes on me, so I turned away from Samantha and gazed around at the different crowds. I saw plenty of other agents I recognized, some even from The Agency, those who worked underneath us, representing other Titans players.

I didn't want to look at any of those fuckers.

They didn't have the body I was after or the mouth I wanted to kiss or the pussy I wanted to bury my tongue inside of.

My attention dragged right back to Samantha.

Fuck this.

"I'll catch you guys in a little bit," I said without waiting for their response, and I began moving toward the right side of the bar.

My cock hardened halfway there, the tip grinding into my suit pants.

This was what she did to me, and I was only staring at her from afar.

By the time I reached her, it was unbearable.

Goddamn it.

I needed it to soften.

I needed to stop imagining the warmth of her cunt.

I needed to push every thought of her out of my head, so I could stare at her lips while she spoke and not think of how soft and wet they were and how hard she had kissed me.

While she faced her sister, I slipped in behind her and pressed into the edge of the counter. "Samantha."

Her body stiffened at the sound of my voice, her head quickly snapping in my direction.

Cinnamon.

I liked that her scent hadn't changed.

"Jack," she whispered.

Shelby leaned around Samantha and said, "Hey, Jack."

I smiled at both women even though only one was returning the gesture. "You girls having a good time?"

"A fantastic time," Shelby said. "My four kids are with a

babysitter, I have a glass of wine in my hand, and my brother won the Super Bowl. It doesn't get much better than that."

I laughed.

Samantha didn't. She stood frozen with her eyes locked on me.

"It's nice that we were all able to attend," Shelby added. "It's just sad that I have to come to my brother's championship game to catch up with this one." She wrapped her arms around Samantha and shook her. "Miss I'm Too Busy to Call Anyone Back."

And then the stare was broken, her face now pointed toward her sister. "Shelby..."

It sounded like a warning.

Shelby released her. "I'm going to go find Dad and make sure he's behaving himself. I'll see you two later."

Samantha opened her mouth to say something, but Shelby walked away before she had a chance.

"Let's get you a refill." I raised my hand in the air, calling over one of the bartenders. When he greeted me, I pointed at Samantha's glass. "Can you top that off?"

He lifted a bottle from behind the bar and held it in front of her, pouring several inches' worth of white wine.

"I really didn't need more," she said once he finished.

"I disagree."

She turned her whole body toward me and searched my eyes.

There was so much happening in hers. More so than I'd ever seen in another woman.

They didn't just speak to me.

They questioned; they demanded.

The only thing I didn't know was what they wanted.

I hoped to fucking hell it was my cock.

Jesus, this situation couldn't get any messier because I still couldn't be with my client's sister.

"I need you to walk away, Jack."

"Can I get you another drink?" the bartender asked.

I looked at him, handing him my empty glass. "Scotch." Then, I glanced back at her. "Is that what you need, or is that what you want?"

6

SAMANTHA

WHAT I NEED?

Is he serious?

It didn't matter how much wine was flowing through my body. Or how hard I'd attempted to focus on what my sister was saying a few minutes ago. Or how excited I was over my brother's game. Or how much I'd tried to distract myself with emails from my clients and vendors.

Nothing had calmed me from the moment I saw Jack outside our suite.

Nothing had made this uneasy feeling go away.

And, now, it was only worse.

He was standing so close.

And he was ridiculously good-looking.

There was no way I could stay in this spot, holding this glass filled with something that only made me more vulnerable, and pretend like I was okay.

Because being around Jack made nothing okay.

I needed air.

Air that didn't have him in it.

"Ladies' room," I blurted out.

I shouldn't have said that. I just knew I had to quickly get away from him, and that was the first thing that had come to me.

I left my wine on the bar and went around the crowd. I had no idea where I was headed. But my eyes were focused on the neon sign that hung from the ceiling, the word *EXIT* shining in bright red.

I pushed myself forward until I reached the door, and then I slammed my palm onto the metal handle and opened it enough where I could slip outside. Before it even shut, I had my back pushed against the building and was sucking in as much air as my lungs could hold.

Jack Hunt was the only man who made it hard for me to breathe. Who made me question the thoughts in my head. Who made me want to shed the thick, hard layer that had grown over my skin even though he was the reason it'd surrounded me in the first place.

My feelings for him should have ended the morning he'd left.

They should have started fresh the moment I'd arrived back in Miami. I should have been crushing over the guys in my dorm, like every other nineteen-year-old in my position.

But Jack had made that impossible.

"Samantha."

My body tightened as I heard his voice through a small crack in the door.

That was the second time he had spoken my name in less than ten minutes, and the emotions it stirred was as intense as when I'd heard it eight years ago.

He moved through the door and stopped in front of me. "Most women don't go outside to use the restroom."

I crossed my arms over my chest. "Why are you out here?"

He opened his mouth, his tongue touching the corner, rubbing the tip back and forth. "I want to talk to you."

"So, you followed me?"

"Wouldn't it have been worse if I'd followed you into the restroom?"

"It would have been better if you hadn't followed me at all."

My stare traveled down to his hand as it went into his pocket.

"Do you want me to leave, Samantha?"

I sighed. "You obviously want something from me, Jack, so why don't you just tell me what it is?"

He smiled.

It was so sexy, I wanted to scream.

"That's where you're wrong." He took a step closer, and then he leaned his side into the building. "I want nothing from you. I just want to be around you."

I pushed harder against the siding, so I wouldn't fall. "Why?"

"Why?" A bit of surprise washed over his face. "Because you're the most beautiful woman I've ever seen."

"Stop."

"It's the truth."

His gaze was too intense, so I shifted my focus to a spot behind him. "You're being ridiculous."

"Look at me, Samantha." He waited until our eyes connected before he said, "I don't lie. I don't have to. You can trust whatever comes out of my mouth. So, when I say you're the most beautiful woman I've ever seen, I fucking mean it." He brought the glass up to his lips, and he swallowed a sip.

I didn't see him move, but suddenly, it felt like he was on top of me.

I held my breath as he stretched his arm over his head, the back of it now resting in the space between us. I felt the breeze it made; I smelled the spiciness of his cologne. He looked down at me where I stood several inches below. Then, he took his fingers out of his pocket and used them to pull a piece of hair off my cheek.

Goddamn it.

Just that little touch sent my body into turmoil, every nerve ending flaring like they were all on fire.

It was his hands.

I remembered how they'd waited for me on the comforter, how several flicks of his finger could almost make me come.

No other hands had made me feel that way since.

But I couldn't let Jack touch me like that again.

I had to stay strong.

I didn't trust myself around him—not my mouth, not my fingers, not my words.

Therefore, I had to get out of here.

"You got what you wanted, and now—"

His eyes turned feral. "I haven't gotten what I wanted. Not even close."

My chest was so tight, the pressure was starting to climb into my throat. "I have to go."

When I tried to take a step away, his hand clasped my cheek, and he dived in closer, his mouth immediately pressing against mine. I took a breath, and I felt his tongue.

My second breath came out as a moan.

And, by the third breath, the memories that involved his lips all came slamming back to me.

He was holding me with so much force and passion that a dampness began to pool between my legs. My body was melting. My skin was begging for his fingers.

But my mind was fighting him.

I couldn't do this.

I had to make him stop.

I pressed my hand to his chest and pushed until he freed me. "How dare you do this now." I was surprised at how emotional I sounded. "You had your chance eight years ago; you're not getting another."

If I said any more, every thought would come pouring out, and I couldn't let that happen.

I also couldn't keep staring at him because the longer I did, the weaker I felt.

"Samantha—"

I put my hand in the air and said, "Jack, don't."

The door was only a few steps behind me, so I rushed toward it and went back inside the bar in search of my sisters to tell them I was going home. Once I did, I would get in the back seat of one of the SUVs my brother had rented for the night, and I would text my best friend, Anna, during the ride home.

Darting around all the groups of people, I found my sisters in the middle of the room, and I saw that they were standing with Shawn.

"There you are," my brother said, resting his arm over my shoulders, dragging me closer to their small circle. "We're doing shots."

I shook my head. "I'm leaving."

He laughed. "No, you're not." He stared at my face as though he were examining me. "You're going to drink; you're way too sober."

"She's *waaay* too sober," my sister, Stacey, slurred. "Open up, little sis. You're getting vodka. Or tequila." She hiccuped. "Or maybe both."

"I definitely don't need both. Or either."

"Shawn, she needs to loosen up," Sara, one of my middle siblings, said.

"Are you guys insane?" I snapped. "I don't need a shot."

Suddenly, there was a bottle dangling over my face, and the metal spout was getting near my lips.

"Shawn, no, I—"

"Have to go?" he said, cutting me off. "You have nowhere to go. I won the fucking Super Bowl today, Sam. Our whole family is here, partying. So, you're going to take a shot with us, and then we're going to have some fun."

I owed him so much for my absence. Taking a shot was the least I could do.

It would probably make me feel a little better and ease some of my anxiety even though I knew Jack was still somewhere inside this bar.

"Sam," Shawn said, "stop thinking, and open your mouth."

When my lips parted, my sisters shouted in celebration.

Shawn tilted the tip of the bottle, and the vodka burned all the way down my throat. But, after the third swallow from a continuous stream of booze that Shawn kept pouring onto my tongue, the knot in my chest began to loosen. Fog filled my head. My limbs turned numb.

But there was one thing I still felt.

One voice I still heard.

One face I still saw in my mind.

No amount of alcohol could ever take that away.

7

SAMANTHA

Anna: You'd better be having a blast right now at the after-party.

Me: Just left. I think I'm drunk.

Anna: Yasss. I want you so hungover tomorrow, you'll be begging me to come over with coffee and five Egg McMuffins.

Me: The thought makes me want to gag.

Anna: Did you have fun?

Me: Jack was there.

Anna: That's no surprise. He told you at the game that he was going to be there.

Me: We talked.

Anna: As in talked, talked? Or just talked?

Me: Don't get crazy.

Anna: How did it go?

Me: It went. He kissed me. It won't happen again.

Anna: Wait, WHAT?

Me: Yeah...

Anna: Hello? You can't just say something like that and not give me any details.

Me: It happened outside, behind the bar. That's where I'd stormed
off after he tried to talk to me the first time.
Anna: I'm confused.
Me: Me, too.
Anna: I take it, this reminded you of how much you'd liked him?
Me: It reminded me of how much he'd hurt me. Now that it's fresh
in my mind again, I can wake up tomorrow morning and pretend
like today never happened.
Anna: We both know tomorrow isn't going to go down that way.
Maybe I need to bring double the amount of Egg McMuffins and
some chocolate cake.
Me: This is why I love you.
Anna: See you at nine.
Me: Ten.
Anna: Oh, please, Lucy isn't going to let you sleep that late.
Me: I'll see you at nine.
Anna: Hey, Sam...
Me: Yeah?
Anna: I'm proud of you.
Me: Shut it. XO

"HI, SAM," Grace, one of the teenagers who lived in the building, said as I walked in the door to my condo.

I reached inside my bag, getting the cash I had stashed in there, and placed it in her hand. "Everything go okay?" I moved back toward the door to walk her out.

"Yep, it went great. If you need me again, call anytime."

I thanked her, locking up after her, and then I switched off most of the lights. As I made my way across the condo, I stopped outside Lucy's door.

She was lying on her stomach in the middle of the bed, knees bent at her sides, her face tucked in somewhere in between. I called it the frog—a position she'd slept in since she was born.

Gently, I ran my fingers through her hair, brushing away the strands from her face. "I love you, baby," I whispered. "I'll see you in the morning. Please let me sleep in."

She stirred and groaned.

I carefully kissed her forehead, making sure not to wake her, and I shut the door behind me, going straight to my room. In my closet, I tossed my jewelry in a drawer and dropped my clothes onto the floor.

I'd deal with it all tomorrow.

Tonight, I needed to be swallowed in a cloud of extra-soft cotton sheets and wrapped in a room full of darkness.

I needed to forget.

But I knew there was no way that could happen.

Even though Jack had never stepped foot in here, this space wasn't free of him.

I felt his presence everywhere.

And, as I climbed into bed, my phone vibrating on the nightstand, I saw his name.

My pulse increased so fast, I felt it pounding in my temples.

It had been eight years since I saw his name on my phone.

Now, five words were written beneath it.

Did you get home safely?

I wondered if he'd kept my number or if he'd asked someone for it. Either way, he had it, and now, I knew his hadn't changed. I was sure he'd switched to a local area code after he moved from LA to Miami. At least that was what I'd told myself, so I never texted him when I was drunk.

It turned out, I was wrong, and I'd had his number all along. That changed nothing.

Because, no matter what, I never would have reached out.

But that didn't help with the position I was in now.

I pulled the blanket over my head and held my phone a few inches from my face.

Responding to him would mean nothing. It would just be words that assured my safety.

It wouldn't be goading him, and it wouldn't imply anything.

Just to be sure, I kept it short.

Yes.

As I stared at what I'd typed, I tried to figure out why I'd never deleted his number. If a part of me had wished he'd reach out at some point. If it was the last thing I had to hold on to, and I just couldn't let him go. If every time I scrolled through my Contacts, I needed to be reminded of the lesson he'd taught me.

I didn't have an answer.

But I knew there was no reason to keep it.

All it would do was tempt me.

And temptation wasn't a good thing when you had a history like ours. When just the tips of his fingers could evoke the most intense passion I'd ever felt. When the scent of him brought back every emotion, every thought, every fear.

So, I went to his Contact page, I clicked Edit, and I scrolled to Delete.

Before I pressed the button, another text from Jack came onto my screen.

It was really good to see you tonight, gorgeous. You tasted as good as I remembered.

I dropped the phone next to me and rolled in the opposite direction.

All the booze in my body should bring me right to sleep.

But I knew there was no way that would ever happen.

8

JACK

I STARED AT MY PHONE, waiting for Samantha's response to come through.

I knew I shouldn't have sent that fucking message, telling her she was gorgeous and how good she'd tasted, but I couldn't help myself. That was how she'd looked tonight, especially after she had some shots with her family and the liquor caused her body to loosen up.

At one point, I'd watched her head tilt back, and a smile filled her face as she laughed. Really laughed, not that fake shit I saw some girls do.

It was almost a relief to see it. Because, whenever I had been close to her, standing next to her at the bar or outside, she was so goddamn uptight, uneasiness covering that beautiful face, tension forcing her body to stiffen.

She was holding a grudge.

I guessed I couldn't blame her. I'd told her once that nothing could ever happen between us, so the last fucking thing I should have been doing was caging her in my arms and kissing her and sending her texts.

I was a contradiction.

But I didn't care.

I wanted her.

Even though I knew how wrong that was.

"Shot?" Scarlett asked, dragging me out of my thoughts. She held a bottle in front of my empty glass and poured, not waiting for my answer.

I didn't know how many fingers' worth of scotch I'd had tonight. I didn't know how many shots I'd slammed back with my friends. But I knew it was going to hurt when I had to get up early tomorrow morning to go to the office.

As I swallowed what Scarlett had put in my tumbler, an email flashed across my screen, catching my attention. It was another contract for Shawn. One that shocked the hell out of me.

"Brett, you've worked with Puma, haven't you?"

He leaned his elbows on the table and nodded. "One of my actresses was signed with them a few years ago."

"They're tricky to work with?"

He laughed. "That's an understatement."

I clicked on my Calendar app and pulled up my schedule. The lines that divided the day into hours were blurry, and the words were, too, so I wasn't able to see my appointments. I'd have my assistant move shit around if I needed.

"You free tomorrow afternoon? I want to talk about your experience with them. It might help if Shawn decides they're worth it."

"Yeah, but you've got to come to my place. My ass isn't going into the office tomorrow."

I held on to the edge of the table. "James must be flying home?"

"Thank fuck. These breaks away from her are brutal."

"I'm sure it's hard, man."

Not that I'd know. I'd never had a long-distance relationship.

Hell, I'd never had anything that lasted more than a few months.

"Do you need me to bring any of your files?" I asked.

He shook his head. "I keep copies of all of them in my home office. I'm sure whatever is there will help you."

"I appreciate it, buddy."

When Max and Scarlett walked away from the table, announcing they were going to the restroom, Brett put his hand on my shoulder. "You want to talk about it? I know you haven't told them, so I was waiting to say something."

"I was trying not to be obvious, but Scarlett busted me staring at Samantha so many fucking times."

He laughed. "She knew something was up when you stopped to talk to her outside their suite. Remember, Scarlett misses nothing."

"Brett, Samantha is the one who got away."

"Fuck. Dramatic much?"

"Don't tell me you didn't feel that way after you spent the night with James the first time."

He put the back of his fist in front of his mouth, like he was going to cough. "Touché, my friend." With his other hand, he pounded my shoulder and released it. "It was a bad idea to pursue James. She was way too fucking young for me. But, back then, I couldn't help myself. I know you're in a similar place. You'll get through it."

I'd been thinking about Samantha since I found out Shawn was going to the Super Bowl.

I couldn't get her out of my head.

And that was before I even saw her again.

Now, that goddamn body of hers was going to consume me. That face was going to haunt me.

Those lips were going to keep me up all fucking night.

"I don't know where the hell I'm at," I told him. "But I know I'm in a rough place."

He took a drink, and after he swallowed, he touched his chest. "Are you feeling that shit in here?"

I sighed. "It's so fucking messy."

"I get it," he said. "You know I do." I watched him glance around the room, his stare landing on Shawn. "I told you to stay away from her back then and to end things, but given what I went through with James, I really had no right to give you that advice. You've got to do what's right for you."

"I don't know what's right for me."

"You know James and I kept our relationship under wraps, so I didn't have people telling me what I should do, and the public wasn't weighing in. Had they known, they would have had a whole lot to say. But, Jack, I wouldn't have listened to one fucking word of it. What I'm trying to say is, you shouldn't listen to anyone else either."

This was on me.

And this decision was on Samantha.

And, right now, I couldn't even get her to text me back.

He emptied his glass and set it on the table. "You ready to get out of here?"

I nodded.

"I'll go grab Max and Scarlett, and I'll meet you out front."

While he walked away, I gazed at the screen of my phone.

One word.

Yes.

That was all she'd given me.

Somehow, I needed to get her to give me more.

9

SAMANTHA

"WAKEY-WAKEY," Anna said as she came into my room the next morning.

I felt around my bed for the nearest pillow, one that wasn't currently under my head, and I threw it over my face. "Go away."

"It hurts?"

"How is it possible that *everything* hurts?"

"Liquor can do that, and you apparently drank way too much of it. That makes me so fucking proud of you."

"Okay, okay," I groaned, pushing the pillow against my ears. Her shouting felt like needles in my eardrums. "I wish you had seen me get Lucy off to school this morning. It was reality-show worthy."

"I would have paid to be here." I heard her move over to me. "Open your eyes. I have lots of treats for you."

"I can smell it."

Even though the conversation was a little hazy, I remembered Anna saying she was going to bring McDonald's for breakfast, and now, the scent of it was filling my room.

"You can't smell the vitamin concoction I made that I swear will cure you."

"I think I need some of that." I gently pulled the pillow off my head and slowly opened my eyes to gradually take in the light. "Ugh."

She handed me a plastic cup with a straw. "You'll feel better once you have something in your stomach. Start with this and then food."

I took a whiff, surprised that it actually smelled pretty good.

I tried sucking through the straw, but it was still too thick, and it made my brain feel like it was going to explode, so I drank straight from the cup.

"Ouch." It even hurt to swallow.

"It'll start feeling better soon, I promise." She climbed into the other side of my bed, covered herself with the comforter, opened one of the McMuffins, and took a bite. "Mmm."

"Good?" Once I had a few gulps down, the coldness coated my throat and made it feel much better.

"Amazing. You don't even have to be hungover to enjoy it."

I held my hand out. "Give me."

"Double-fisting. That's my girl."

I took the sandwich and unwrapped it halfway, biting from the top. "Oh my."

"I'm right, aren't I?"

I didn't even bother to cover my mouth when I said, "This is one of the most incredible things I've ever eaten."

"Don't worry; there are four more in the bag."

I laughed despite how much it hurt, and I leaned back against my headboard. "What the hell happened last night? I'm almost afraid to look at my phone to see all the drunk pictures my family took."

"Well...I know you kissed Jack. What didn't happen was, you going back to his place to get it on."

"I..." My voice faded as the events of last night began to emerge through the fog.

Jack at the game, Jack at the after-party, Jack talking to me at the bar, Jack following me outside.

Jack's lips on mine.

Jack texting me when I got home.

"Ugh," I repeated.

She turned toward me while she chewed. "I had a feeling you'd remember that part."

"Maybe I should go back to sleep to see if I can forget it again."

"Not a chance. We have good shit to eat. Coffee to drink. And we have lots of Jack to talk about."

Ignoring her, I lifted my phone off the nightstand and scrolled through the messages on the lock screen. There were too many to process, and my brain wasn't fully functioning yet, so I clicked directly on the Messages app.

Four texts down, I saw his name.

I saw his words.

Gorgeous.

Tasted.

Good.

I immediately tossed it back on the nightstand.

"I think we need to discuss this," she said.

I filled my mouth with a large bite. "That man can't come back into my life like no time has passed, like he didn't just throw me away. He can't, Anna. He just can't," I spoke through the Canadian bacon and the cheese and the egg, and I did nothing to try to hide it because I needed it in my stomach as much as I needed to get this out.

"I know why you feel that way, but—"

"Rewinding is the only way this could ever work. But I can't go back, and neither can he, so we're wasting our time even thinking about this."

Even if I'll consider it, does Jack deserve me?

I'd tried endlessly to reach out to him through texts and phone calls, even telling him I needed to talk to him, and he ignored every attempt. Then, he'd cut things off like I meant nothing to him.

"You were kids back then."

I turned in the bed, feeling pieces of egg fall onto my chest. "Are you really sticking up for him?"

"No. Yes. Maybe a little."

"I know you're not saying what I think you are." I could barely get the words out because I was in complete disbelief she could even suggest this.

She shrugged.

"So, you are being serious?"

"Sam, you obviously felt something for him last night, and it rekindled all the emotions you'd had from years ago. You might have pushed those feelings aside, and maybe they lightened, but I know they never went away." She took another Egg McMuffin out of the bag and set it in front of me. "Thinking about Jack isn't a waste of time. This is your life, your past, and possibly your future."

Anna and I had been best friends since we were five. Of course she was inside my head, reading my thoughts and trying to organize them for me.

Still, that didn't change the obvious.

"You're crazy. And I'm not just saying that because I'm hungover. This conversation is fucked on every level."

"Listen to me." She waited until I looked at her. "There's a reason you saw Jack yesterday and why he gave you so much attention. There's also a reason he kissed you. So, why not keep an open mind and see what happens?"

"Because—"

She put her hand up to stop me from answering. "All I'm saying is, things have a funny way of working out sometimes. Who knows what could come of it?"

Anna had been at the University of Florida when I met Jack. I called her from LaGuardia before my flight took off to tell her all about my night with him. And, when he ended things, I drove to Gainesville, so I could sob on her shoulder.

She was the one to pick up all the pieces.

My pieces.

And, slowly, she'd helped me glue myself back together.

Now, she wanted me to revisit it? Go back to that place where he had hurt me so badly? Repair a history that was so marred with scars?

But it wasn't just me anymore.

There was Lucy to think about, too.

I took a breath, trying to process everything that had been said, and I was interrupted by an alarm that came across my phone. I checked the screen, and it showed I had an appointment in thirty minutes.

Not just any appointment.

A meeting with James Ryne and Brett Young to discuss their house in LA.

"Oh, shit." I threw the blanket off, watching the sandwich go flying, and I rushed into the bathroom.

"Um, what's going on?"

Knowing I didn't have time to shower, I ran my hands under the faucet and then pressed my wet fingers under my eyes to wash off yesterday's makeup. "I'm supposed to be at James Ryne's condo in thirty."

"Yikes."

"Now, you see why I'm manic right now."

"How long will it take you to get there?"

"Five-ish minutes." I patted my face with a towel and lathered on some concealer. "They only live a few buildings over."

"You'll be fine then."

I grabbed a blush brush and swished it across the middle of my cheeks. "Time-wise, probably. I just wish I weren't so hungover. She's hiring me to design an entire house, and I have so much to discuss with her."

"Can you reschedule?"

I laughed and gripped the sides of my head to stop the stabbing pain. "No. Not even a chance. I've been waiting my whole career for a project like this with someone as wonderful as her. Somehow, I need to get my shit together and act as though I'm not dying on the inside."

"Sam?"

I stopped swiping the mascara wand over my eyelashes to glance in her direction. "Yeah?"

"Don't forget to brush your teeth."

"Oh God."

I finished coating my lashes and slathered some toothpaste on my toothbrush. "That would have been scary," I said, although I was pretty sure she couldn't understand me while I was scrubbing my teeth.

"Girl, you've got this. You just had a few too many cocktails last night. I mean, your brother did win the Super Bowl. I'm sure she'll understand."

I washed my mouth out. "She doesn't know Shawn is my brother." After drying my lips, I went into my closet and put on a pair of skinny jeans and a tank that I covered with a blazer. Then, I finished the outfit with a pair of sky-high heels. I tossed on plenty of jewelry and went back into the bathroom to put my hair in a ponytail. Once I was done, I moved over to the bed. "How do I look?"

"She doesn't know Shawn's your brother? Really?"

"Her fiancé is partners with Jack. I really didn't want to go there."

"Jesus."

"I know." I twirled in a circle, going extremely slow so that I wouldn't get sick. "We can talk about all of that later. Right now, I need to know how I look."

"For being unshowered, dousing yourself in perfume, and forgetting to put panties on, I'd say you're hot as fuck."

"I forgot to put panties on?" I reached inside my jeans. "Wow. I did."

"There's no time to bother with that now. Go get the stuff you need, and get out the door."

I went into my closet, picked up my workbag, and slung it over my shoulder. When I got to the doorway, I looked behind me just as she took a bite of her Egg McMuffin. "I'm seething in jealousy at the moment."

"Don't. Once your meeting is over, you can rejoin me because I don't plan on moving while you're gone. Then, we can pick up right where we left off."

"What about the breakfast?"

"I'll put the leftovers in the fridge. You can gorge when you get home."

I kissed the air and winced from the sharp movement. "You're the best."

"Brett, this is Samantha Laine," James said as she walked me into the kitchen where he was getting some coffee.

Brett turned around, and our eyes connected. He paused for several seconds, as though he were trying to place me. I saw the moment he did, a smile spreading across his whole face.

"Samantha, it's nice to see you again. Are you feeling as hungover as me?"

I shook his hand, knowing my answer should stay professional even though it would be a lie. "I'm doing okay."

"You two saw each other last night?" James asked.

My chest filled with anxiety, as I knew the truth was about to come out.

"The guys and I stopped by her parents' suite to congratulate them, and then I saw her at the after-party."

"Are your parents partial owners of one of the teams?" she asked.

I opened my mouth, but Brett beat me to it.

"Baby, Samantha's brother is Shawn Cole, the starting tight end for Tennessee and one of our clients." He looked at me. "You don't go by Cole?"

I took a deep breath, eyeing the mug of coffee in his hand. If I wasn't so queasy, I would be craving a cocktail to ease some of this nervousness, but right now, I just needed something to dull this headache, and caffeine could really help. "Professionally, no, I use my mother's maiden name. But, personally, yes, I'm Samantha Cole."

"Samantha, I feel so foolish. I had no idea your brother was connected to The Agency, but I'm thrilled to hear it," James said.

"Oh no, please don't feel foolish, and please don't be offended that I didn't say anything. I just try to keep family and work completely separate."

She put her hand on my arm. "Believe me, I understand." She looked at Brett. "We both do."

I was so relieved she wasn't upset or sketched out by my name change.

Now that all that drama was out of the way, I wanted to move on to why I was here.

More anxiety started to fill my chest. "Is there a place you want to sit, so I can show you some of the designs?"

"Yes, of course. How about the kitchen table?" As she signaled me to follow her, she said, "Brett, do you mind grabbing Samantha some coffee?" She smiled at me. "If you're feeling like Brett right now, I'm sure you could use some."

I nodded. "I appreciate it."

Once we got to the space, I opened my bag and took out the stack of drawings. It had taken me weeks to put these together, pulling several all-nighters just to get them the way I wanted.

"Cream? Sugar?" Brett asked.

"Just black, thank you."

I'd put the drawings in a special order when I packed them into my bag, so I lifted the first one off the pile and held it in my hands, waiting for Brett to join us. Once he set the mug in front of me, I thanked him again, and he took a seat across from me.

"We're going to start with the most personal room in the house." I placed the board on the table and pushed it toward them. "This is how I envision your bedroom."

"Oh my God," James said as she stared at the sketch.

I held my breath, waiting to hear the rest of her reaction and Brett's, who remained silent.

Since I'd done work in this condo, I already knew his taste. My goal was to combine his style with James's, throwing in both masculine and feminine colors and accessories while keeping the space soft and light where relaxation was the key theme.

It hadn't been easy.

"Both closets can be adjusted any way you want them," I said. "I just wanted you to see the location of each, the size, and possibilities. Also worth noting is that the ratio of sleeping to lounging space in the main room can be increased or decreased, depending on how much you want of each."

James looked at Brett, and he gave her a nod. Then, the both of them glanced at me.

"I'm in love with it," she said. "All of it."

Even though the sickness in my stomach was still there, I felt like I could finally take a deep breath without the tightness in my chest holding me back.

"It's good, Samantha," he said. "Real good."

I let myself smile but only briefly before pulling out the second board and setting it in front of them. "Here's the man cave."

Brett's gaze moved to James. "We didn't discuss a man cave."

"I know, babe. I wanted to surprise you. What do you think?"

He shook his head, his teeth gnawing on his lip. "I think it's perfect." His stare moved to me. "Now, I see why James loves you. You've got one hell of an eye for this."

Brett didn't seem like the kind of guy who gave compliments easily. Because of that, his words meant everything to me.

Trying not to let the emotion come through my voice, I said, "Thank you," and then I placed another board in front of them. "Here's the movie theater."

"Fuck," he said. "I didn't think it could get better than what you'd shown me." As he looked up, all the anxiety left my body, and it was replaced with excitement. "But it just did."

10

JACK

Brett: *You're not going to believe this shit.*
Me: *I'm hungover as fuck. I'd believe just about anything
right now.*
Brett: *Samantha is our interior designer. She's in my house,
meeting with us about our place in LA.*
Me: *You didn't know you'd hired her?*
Brett: *I'd never met her until this morning.*
Me: *Christ. I didn't even know she did that for a living.*
Brett: *You busy now? I'd say it's the perfect time to come over to
talk about Puma.*
Me: *I'll be right there.*
Brett: *I'll stall her if I have to.*
Me: *Good man.*

11

SAMANTHA

I PLACED the final sketch on the table and slid it over to James and Brett. This board showed the backyard where I'd designed a summer kitchen, two large seating areas, a fire pit, and a pool. "The colors I used in the living room were also incorporated outside." I moved the drawing of the living room right next to it, so they could see them side by side. "I want the interior to flow seamlessly into the outdoor space. My idea was to go for a spa, Zen-like feel."

"It's stunning," James said. "Magical even. I can't believe we're going to own something so beautiful."

So far, they liked everything I'd shown them, and structurally, they didn't have any changes. However, certain additions had been discussed for several of the rooms, and I would work in those elements and send them updated designs.

James looked up from the drawing and said, "Samantha, I'm so blown away by everything right now; I don't even know what to say."

"I do," Brett came back with while looking at his fiancée. "You're making James fall in love with the house so much, she's

83

going to want to move there permanently." He glanced at me. "I can't have that. My business is here. So, you need to do me a favor, Samantha. The next set of sketches you bring need to really suck."

"Brett!" She gently punched his arm. "LA is work. Miami is home. I've told you that since I moved here. Samantha's designs, despite how incredible they are, won't change that." She gave him a quick kiss and then gazed at me. "One day, I'll convince Brett to move out of this condo and into a house, and we'll get to start this process all over."

"Jesus," Brett groaned.

She laughed. "You can tell he's terribly excited about that."

"You have a gorgeous home here," I assured the both of them. "And a lovely place in LA that will serve as a nice getaway." I brought the coffee mug to my lips, and just as I took the last sip, I heard the soft buzz of the elevator.

"Hey, hey," a man said from the entryway, the sound of feet now moving across the floor.

Jack.

I would recognize his voice anywhere.

The anxiety, which had been gone since I received Brett's compliments, was back and seizing my chest. Tingles were spreading throughout my whole body. There was a tightening in the back of my throat.

I held my breath, turning around in my chair, waiting for Jack to appear in the kitchen.

I shouldn't be surprised he was here. He was partners with Brett after all. What surprised me was how the simple sound of his voice caused such a reaction inside me, a war erupting in my mind with no resolution in sight.

"Good morning, Jack," James said, obviously recognizing his voice, too, since he still hadn't emerged.

"Morning," he replied back.

I sucked in another breath, and that was when he appeared.

Our eyes locked.

Dark gray suit. Black tie. That sexy beard covering some of his face.

God, he was so ridiculously good-looking.

"Grab yourself some coffee," Brett said to him.

"Nah, I'm good."

Jack went over to James and gave her a hug. Then, he clasped Brett's hand, leaning into his chest where they patted each other's backs. Finally, he came to me, moving in fast to kiss me on the cheek.

That scent.

Those rough whiskers.

The softness of his lips.

It was impossible to calm what was happening inside me.

If James or Brett were watching me, I was sure my face was giving away exactly how Jack made me feel. And, if Jack noticed, I was sure he was loving every second of it.

"I didn't know you were stopping by this morning," James said as Jack sat in the chair next to mine.

He crossed his arms. "Brett has some files I need to look at for one of my clients."

"Do you need to go?" she asked Brett.

He shook his head. "I don't think Jack's in a rush."

"I'm not," Jack replied.

Since we were done with our meeting and it sounded like the boys had some things they needed to discuss, I grabbed my bag from the back of my chair and lifted it onto my shoulder. "I've kept you long enough. I'm going to leave the drawings here, so you have them, and once I have updated designs, I'll schedule another appointment with you."

"Sounds wonderful," James said.

I smiled at her before extending my hand toward Brett. "It

was really nice to officially meet you."

His grip was firm. "It was a real pleasure, Samantha."

"I'll walk her out," Jack offered.

Neither Brett nor James said anything. I didn't want to fight him on it, especially not here and in front of them, so I stayed silent as I moved out of the kitchen and into the foyer, immediately stepping into the open elevator.

Once he got in and the door shut, I said, "Did you know I was here?"

"Brett told me."

"So, you knew this whole time that I've been designing for them."

He shook his head. "No, I just found out today. Brett didn't know either until he saw you this morning."

I moved to the other wall, opposite him. "You have no concept of boundaries, Jack. You really need to stop following me."

He faced me, reaching behind him to hold the railing. "Samantha, I'll go anywhere to talk to you even if that means coming to my best friend's house. I wanted to see you. I heard you were here, so I came over."

"Don't you know how wrong that is?"

He smiled. It was so sexy, it almost hurt.

"You're all I think about. Don't ever call that wrong."

"Jack, we—"

"Have dinner with me tonight."

His suggestion was so casual; it was like we'd been dating for years.

I laughed. "No."

"Why? You have plans?" He didn't wait for me to respond. "I'm flying out tomorrow to go to Nashville to meet with your brother, so I'll be gone for a few days. Have dinner with me tonight."

ENDORSED

I'd gone out last night for the Super Bowl, and now, he was asking me to go out tonight. I'd have to find someone else to watch Lucy; I couldn't ask Grace for back-to-back evenings since she had school, too. When work tried dragging me away during weeknights, I always fought it. Being home for Lucy was my top priority, and tonight was no exception.

"No."

His stare narrowed. "Please."

"Why do you want to have dinner with me, Jack?"

"Because we both need to eat. Why not do it together?"

"You're still my brother's agent."

His smile grew. It wasn't mocking me at all. It was doing the opposite. "It's just dinner, Samantha. Don't let your mind wander; don't overthink it. Two people, sitting at a table, enjoying food together. That's it."

"But why now, after all these years, do you want to see me so badly?"

"Because I can't get you out of my head. Because seeing you again brought back everything I'd felt eight years ago, but this time, it came back even stronger."

I needed to get out of this elevator and away from him because he was clouding my judgment.

"I'm supposed to meet with a client tonight," I lied. "Let me see if I can get the meeting moved, and I'll let you know."

The door opened as we reached the lobby. I stayed on my side of the elevator, far from his hands, and slipped out. I wasn't more than a few steps away when he called my name.

I turned around.

"Just say yes."

I took a deep breath, the sound of his voice hitting me in a place where it shouldn't. "I'll text you."

I faced the front door and walked through it, rushing down the sidewalk toward my building.

87

Surprisingly, my hangover was gone, which probably was due to the coffee and the vitamin shake and the egg sandwich.

But I still didn't feel right, and it was because of Jack.

I'd avoided my brother's games, so there was no chance I'd run into him. Now that I had seen him again, it had gone so much further than I ever expected. And, now, I was faced with a decision.

One that didn't become any clearer as I opened the door to my condo. I dropped my bag in the entryway and went straight to my bedroom, kicking off my heels and climbing into bed.

Anna's eyes popped open, as she'd been napping. "How'd it go?"

I picked a piece of egg off the comforter. "Jack showed up."

"You're fucking kidding me."

I turned my head toward her. "I can't even make that up."

"And?"

"He wants to have dinner."

"And?"

"Do you know any word besides *and*?"

She grinned. "AND?"

"I told him I'd text him to let him know."

With my phone uncomfortably resting in my back pocket, I slipped it out and set it on my nightstand. "I'd have to ask my parents to take Lucy tonight and—"

"I'll watch Lucy."

"No, you don't have to do that. I'm just going to tell Jack I can't have dinner. I'm really not sure it's a good idea for me to go anyway."

"Samantha."

Anna never called me by my full name, so I knew whatever she was about to say was going to be serious.

"Don't think about what happened. Just hear him out, and

focus on what kind of guy he is. You know, if you don't do this, you'll never forgive yourself."

I hated when she was right.

Especially now.

"So, you're saying I should—"

"First, you're going to pick up your phone and text him that you're in for dinner." She sat up in the bed, looking as bossy as she sounded. "Then, we're going to plan your outfit and get you ready. Finally, I'm going to stay here and watch your kid. You have zero excuses; don't try to come up with one."

I pushed my head back into the pillow. "Really?"

"Just fucking text him already."

I rolled my eyes and reached toward the nightstand, pulling my cell phone into my hand. I opened the last text from him, and I started to type.

Me: Tell me where to meet you.
Jack: I'll forward you the reservation.
Jack: Samantha?
Me: What?
Jack: Thank you.

12

SAMANTHA

EVEN THOUGH I could see Jack from the entrance of the restaurant, sitting in the back corner of the dining room, the hostess insisted on escorting me to his table. So, I walked behind her, feeling the moment when his eyes connected with my body, which was only a few steps in, and he continued to watch me as I made my way across the large space.

I wanted him to question whether or not I would show.

I wanted him to look in my direction as I approached the table, wearing my favorite black dress that hugged every curve I had, that showed my small amount of cleavage, so he could see what he'd given up.

Those were the reasons I had arrived a few minutes late and why I had told Jack I'd meet him here instead of accepting his offer to pick me up.

As I reached him, he stood and kissed me on the cheek. "You look gorgeous," he whispered in my ear.

He'd told me to believe everything he said.

From the way he was looking at me, from the intensity of his gaze, it was impossible not to.

I tried to stop myself from blushing, and I took the seat across from his.

He was wearing a different suit than he'd had on earlier. This one was black, and he'd paired it with a matching solid tie that was incredibly sexy. He'd shaved under his chin, so his beard looked a little more refined.

"Have you eaten here before?" he asked.

Pappardelle was one of my favorite restaurants in Miami. There was no way he could have known that, so him choosing it had to be a coincidence. One that I definitely noted.

I placed my napkin in my lap. "Many times."

"Then, you must like it here."

"Very much."

He paused for several seconds, his thumb tracing the drips of water running down his glass. "I appreciate you rearranging your schedule to join me."

Those goddamn fingers.

They made me quiver.

Enough where I couldn't think of anything to say back to him.

Fortunately, I was saved by the waiter.

"Welcome to Pappardelle. My name is Alvin, and I'll be taking care of you tonight. Can I start you off with something to drink?"

As I reached for the wine menu in the middle of the table, Jack said, "I'll take a bottle of the Domaine J.F. Mugnier pinot noir." His eyes never left mine.

Jack knew he didn't have to impress me with his success. I was well aware of how much money he made off my brother, and Shawn was just one of his many clients. Therefore, the three-hundred-dollar bottle of wine he'd just ordered was because he liked it and because he had excellent taste.

I broke our stare to look at the waiter. "Two glasses, please."

ENDORSED

He nodded and disappeared from our table.

Jack's gaze turned even deeper.

Feeling the need to break the silence, I said the first thing that came to me, "I didn't peg you as a wine drinker."

He rested his elbows on the table and leaned in closer. "I have a wide range of taste when it comes to alcohol."

"How did you know I didn't want white?"

He rubbed across his bottom lip. "Something tells me you like white for social settings because it's light and easy. When you want to enjoy what you're drinking or you're dining, you like red."

The only thing Jack Hunt had known about me was how to make me come.

But that was no longer true. He'd just pointed out something that not even Anna ever picked up on.

"Am I right?"

I shrugged.

"Samantha, agreeing with me doesn't mean you're caving. This isn't a point system. No matter what, you're always going to win. I was in the wrong; I think we've already established that."

I wasn't keeping score.

I was just trying to keep it together.

"Have we, Jack?"

The waiter then returned to the table, holding the wine. He showed the label to Jack, who nodded in approval, and the waiter poured him a taste. Once Jack swallowed the small amount, he nodded once more, and the waiter filled both glasses.

Jack held his up in the air. "Should we toast?"

I swirled the wine around and gripped the stem. "I think you should."

"To eight years later." He smiled, and my teeth immediately sank into my bottom lip. "And to the three days I spent with you that I still haven't forgotten."

93

I hadn't either.

I clinked against his glass and took a sip, the sides of my tongue bursting from all the different notes in the wine.

Once his hands were free, he said, "I take it, you don't accept my apology?"

I almost laughed. "What apology? You mean, the *I'm sorry* you sent in the text? Do me a favor and remind me never to fight with you because, if that's what you consider heartfelt, then I'll live in a constant state of disappointment."

"Samantha—"

"Can I start you with any appetizers?" the waiter said.

I hadn't even seen him come back to the table.

Jack looked at me for an answer, but my menu was still resting on the charger. Unopened.

"How about you bring us some calamari and a caprese salad?" Jack said.

"I'll put those right in," he replied.

Jack waited until we were alone again before he said, "Listen to me, I didn't want things between us to end that way, but I knew, if I called you and heard your voice, I would have changed my mind, and I would have been on the next flight to Miami. That wouldn't have been good for either of us."

"Why?"

"I was twenty-three years old. I didn't know how to treat a woman properly or how to be in a relationship, especially one that would have been bicoastal. Back then, I was in no position to go to Shawn and tell him how much I liked you. I had just become an agent. Your brother was one of the first clients I'd signed, and he trusted me with his career. He needed all of my focus. What he didn't need was to worry that I was spending more time thinking about his sister than him." He shook his head, looking at the table for just a second. "I never wanted him to question my integrity or my ambition. I had a lot to prove and a lot to learn. And I've done both."

"That doesn't make it right."

"No, it doesn't. I'm ashamed of the way I treated you. You didn't deserve that, and I wish I could take it back. I understand why you're upset with me."

He understood nothing.

"So, the first time you see me after all these years, you decide you want to start spending time with me? It's a little late, isn't it?"

"Late?" The heaviness on his face started to lift, and the playfulness I'd seen eight years ago was hinting its way back. "No, I don't think it's too late. I asked you to have dinner with me. You came. Now, we have a lot to catch up on, and I want to hear it all." He took a drink of his wine. "Fill me in."

"I graduated from the University of Miami, I interned, and I worked for a local design company until I went off on my own. That pretty much sums it up."

"I know you didn't use your brother to get through any doors. Hell, you even changed your last name, so that tells me you did it all on your own. And, now, you have clients like James Ryne, one of the highest-paid actresses in the world. You're twenty-seven years old, Samantha. That's some impressive shit."

His compliments made me feel a little emotional. I wasn't sure why. "It's been a journey."

"Sounds like it."

It was one I'd done without any financial help from my brother. Besides some free babysitting from my parents and sisters—before I could actually afford a sitter—that was about as much assistance as I'd allowed my family to give me.

I wanted to build a good life for Lucy and me.

And I was determined to do it on my own.

"You've done so well for yourself." His smile returned. "It's really good to see."

"I can say the same about you."

The waiter came back with the appetizers and set them between us. "Are you ready to order your main course?"

"I think we need a few minutes. She hasn't had a chance to look yet," Jack said.

"No, I'm ready." I handed my menu to the waiter. "I'll have the eggplant parmesan with a side of penne."

"And for you, sir?"

Jack's smile grew as he looked at me. "Veal parmesan with a side of penne."

"I'll put those right in." He topped off each of our wine glasses before he left.

"How many times have you had their eggplant?" Jack asked me.

"I've never eaten anything else here." Since I hadn't seen him open his menu either, I guessed his answer. "Same with the veal?"

"Once I find something I love, it's over."

That was an interesting choice of words, but I agreed with him.

I used my fork to swipe a ring of calamari, and I popped it into my mouth.

"Will you have dinner with me again when I get back from Nashville?"

I put my hand over my lips while I was still chewing. "Jack, we haven't even finished this dinner yet."

"I'm already thinking about the next time I'm going to see you."

I set my fork down and swallowed. "I don't know."

"Why the hesitation?" He moved his legs underneath the table, and his toes briefly touched mine. "Because, if we're just talking about food, then there's no reason you can't eat with me."

"We both know this isn't about food."

The crinkles around his eyes deepened, same with the ones in his forehead. "You're the one who got away."

"You let me."

"I want you back."

I reached for my wine and took several sips, hoping it would kick in quickly. I had known this conversation was going to happen; I just hadn't known that it was going to affect me this hard. "That isn't up to you."

"That's why we're only starting with dinner, and that decision is up to you."

"Why is this time so different?"

"I told you, Samantha, I'm not the twenty-three-year-old you met in New York. I've had eight years to grow up. To learn what I want. To put my priorities together and figure out how to be a man you'd want to be with." While he paused, I tried to process what he was saying, tried to look past the blue of his eyes that were practically mesmerizing me. "Another reason this time will be different is that I'll talk to your brother about it while I'm in Nashville. If I'm going to take you out, I want to come clean, and I want to get his approval."

I felt my back shoot up straight, panic immediately plunging into my chest. "You mean, you're going to tell him about New York?"

"Fuck no. I'm going to tell him I like you, and I want to spend time with you." His finger grazed mine, and that was when I realized I was still holding my wine glass. I felt his touch all the way down in my toes. "I don't want to have to hide my feelings or keep them a secret."

I couldn't believe what I was hearing.

My head felt like it was going to explode.

My heart wasn't too far behind it.

"Say something," he demanded.

His big, beautiful eyes were still staring at me, urging my feelings forward.

Eyes that I'd never forgotten.

Eyes that I couldn't forget.

"I don't know, Jack."

I couldn't just let him right back in my life.

He'd crushed me. That didn't mean he deserved a second chance the minute he resurfaced and told me he'd changed.

But I could picture us eating together a second time. I could also imagine the hurt I would feel if I left this restaurant and never saw him again.

"Dinner," I said. "That's all I'm agreeing to right now."

"I'm not asking for more."

But, if more was in our future, then his entire world was about to change.

Because it wasn't just me anymore.

I was a mother, and Lucy would always come first.

She was my entire world.

A world I wasn't ready to tell him about just yet.

13

JACK

WITH MY HAND lightly touching Samantha's lower back, I walked her to the front of the restaurant and handed the valet the ticket for my car. Since she made no effort to do the same, I assumed she hadn't used valet and said, "Where'd you park?"

"I didn't. I got dropped off." She reached into her small bag and pulled out her phone. "I'm going to just use my app to get a car to take me home."

I put my hand on her arm to stop her from typing. "I'll give you a ride."

I had no idea where she lived, but I'd drive to fucking Orlando if that meant I could spend more time with her.

"No, don't worry; it'll take me only two seconds to get a car."

"Samantha, let me do it."

I saw the hesitation in her eyes.

It wasn't any different than how she'd looked when she first sat down at the table or when I'd asked her to go to dinner with me again.

She was being cautious.

I respected that.

The driver pulled my car up to the curb, got out, and stood next to the open door.

I gazed at Samantha, waiting for her decision. "Are you coming with me?" I asked when she still hadn't said anything but was no longer typing on her screen.

"I guess so."

I went to the passenger door and opened it for her. Once she got settled, I shut it and went to my side of the car, shifting into first gear before driving off.

"Where do you live?"

"I'm on Biscayne Boulevard, right past the corner of northeast Tenth Street."

"Ah, that's easy."

And it was close by.

What she didn't know was that she lived by me as well.

I wouldn't tell her that. I'd given her enough information tonight to process.

When I stopped at the first light, she asked, "What time is your flight tomorrow?"

"I have to check, but I think my assistant scheduled the pilots for eight in the morning." I glanced at her. "You should come. You can hang out with your brother when I'm not meeting with him. There's plenty of room on the plane."

The thought of having her on The Agency's private jet made my dick start to harden. That delicious body, over thirty thousand feet in the air, with a back bedroom that would be so perfect to fuck her in.

She shook her head. "I have way too much work to do."

Samantha's dedication to her job was sexy as hell, and it made me think my schedule wouldn't bother her at all. There weren't many girls like that. All the ones I'd met did nothing but bitch about how often I traveled.

"When do you come back?"

The light turned green, and I stepped on the gas. "I'll be gone for only two nights." As I shifted into second, I stole a glance at her. "Why? Are you going to miss me?"

"You're relentless."

"Nah. I just want you."

I knew it wasn't a reflection from the brake lights ahead of us that caused her face to redden. It was from my words, and I fucking loved seeing her react that way to me.

I weaved through a back street that brought me to the side of Brett's place, and then I took my final turn, knowing she was just a few buildings down.

"That one," she said, pointing at the white stucco.

Instead of driving up to the front, I parked several car lengths away in a spot that wasn't under a streetlight and shifted into neutral before I turned off the car. "I'll let you pick the restaurant next time."

With one hand on her seat belt and another on the handle of the door, she turned her face toward me. "I would have chosen Pappardelle."

"We can go back there."

"It's okay; we'll save it for another time."

I reached forward and cupped her cheek. I could tell the gesture surprised her, but I couldn't help myself. I needed to touch her. "So, you're saying the next dinner won't be our last?"

She smiled even though it was subtle. "I make no promises."

Her body was telling me a much different story.

Her chest was rising and falling much faster than it needed to. Her legs were swishing back and forth, like she was trying to rub out the tension.

I was sure she didn't even realize she was doing it.

But I did.

And between those thighs was the only place I wanted to be right now.

"Can I make you a promise, Samantha?"

"Yes."

"Before you get out of this car, you're going to come." I held her tighter, so she knew I was serious.

"Jack..."

I moved my face toward her and stopped when I was inches away. "I want you to kiss me." She took a breath, and I could almost taste the nervousness when she exhaled. "I meant what I said in the restaurant; I want you back. So, stop thinking, listen to what your body wants, and let me take care of it for you."

She quickly looked out the windshield and then through the passenger window. "We're in your car. Are you just going to—"

"Kiss me."

"What if someone walks by and sees us?"

"The glass is tinted. No one can see anything."

I felt the war that was raging inside her head, the one where she was fighting with herself over what she wanted and what she felt was right.

My hands were what she wanted.

But taking this slow was what she felt was right.

Before she said anything, she had to know this, "You can trust me."

While I waited for her lips, I dipped mine into her neck, on the spot right underneath her jaw. I remembered that being a sensitive place on her body. I'd remembered correctly because, the second I pressed down, she let out the softest moan. And she did once again when I moved closer to her throat.

My dick was hard long before my mouth had gotten anywhere near her. Now, it was fucking throbbing, the tip grinding into my zipper, my balls begging for a release.

"Samantha," I groaned.

With my free hand, I released her seat belt. Then, I gently touched the other side of her neck, keeping my fingers loose, so I could run them down her body. She felt amazing in this dress, her tits pushed together by the tight fabric, her thin waist and the dip of her hips outlined underneath the material.

I needed more of her.

I dropped down to her shoulder and gradually to her side, sliding across her thigh and coming to a stop in the middle of it, halfway from her pussy and knee.

"Jack," she moaned, my mouth now on her cheek.

"Kiss me."

She turned her face. Her lips were right in front of mine, parted. Her eyes were so goddamn hungry.

I needed to know she wanted this.

"Kiss me," I repeated.

She looked at my mouth and seemed to take it in before she closed the distance between us. My tongue glided through, circling the tip of hers, our lips intertwined.

Fuck, she tasted good.

Now, I needed to know how she felt.

The edge of her dress sat just above her knees. I slipped my fingers underneath it, pushing her legs apart as I moved my way up to her pussy. A piece of lace fabric was the only thing that kept me from diving into her warmth. Just as I slid it to the side, she gripped my wrist.

"Do you want me to stop?"

"No." She breathed. "I want to feel your fingers."

I didn't think my cock could get harder than it already was.

I was so fucking wrong.

With her still holding my hand, knowing she could now feel my movements from both sides, I went underneath the fabric.

It wasn't just heat that met my fingers.

"Samantha," I hissed, "you're so wet."

Her head tilted back, and I kissed her throat as I rubbed up and down, spreading the wetness, letting her get used to my touch again.

I missed this fucking pussy.

The tightness of it.

The softness of her skin.

The way those two perfect lips surrounded the present I wanted to swipe with my tongue.

Each time I lowered, she would squeeze my wrist. Her need to come was building, the longer I held her off.

"*Ahhh*," she moaned when I wedged my fingers between her lips and gave just a little more pressure to that sensitive spot at the very top. "Jack..."

The sound of my name coming from her mouth was my undoing.

I slipped inside her, going up to both knuckles, and I put my thumb on her clit.

"Oh my God," she groaned, the words vibrating through her throat. "Your hands."

I plunged into her pussy, using the same speed as I ground into the top. She was still leaning into the headrest, her throat fully exposed, so I kissed up and down her neck, sucking a little harder in some spots, just not enough to leave a mark.

I knew she was close.

Her sounds were filling my car.

Her wetness was coating my skin.

Her nails were digging into me.

When I felt her clench, I took my thumb and shifted it back and forth as fast as I could, my two fingers staying buried to grind out her orgasm.

She bucked her hips forward, her back pushing into the seat, her hand holding my wrist like I was going to stop.

But there was no way I could.

As good as I was making her feel, she was making me feel even better.

"Jack," she moaned one last time.

Her pussy tightened around me until I felt her shudder, a series of ripples that started inside her cunt and worked through her navel.

It was the hottest fucking thing I'd ever seen.

"Kiss me," I demanded one final time.

She gave me her lips, and I devoured them until her body stilled, my fingers gently sliding out, my hand lifting from beneath her dress.

She released my wrist but kept her eyes on it.

Even though it was dark in my car, I could still see the glistening on my skin. Knowing she was watching me, I brought my hand up to my mouth, and I licked every spot that had been inside her. "I've been waiting a long time to do that."

And to kiss every inch of her skin.

And to eat her pussy.

And to fuck her.

I hoped I would get the chance soon.

"Your hands have only gotten better," she said.

"They're yours. Whenever you want them."

She said nothing for several seconds, and then she reached for the door handle. "I have to go."

"Samantha," I said before she shut the door behind her, "I'm going to make this right."

She didn't respond. She just closed the door and went inside her building.

14

SAMANTHA

I SHUT the door to Jack's sports car and rushed into the lobby of my building, waiting for the elevator to open before I hurried inside and pushed the button to my floor. Once the door slid shut, I leaned my back against the wall and tried to find my breath.

Inhaling through my nose and exhaling out of my mouth wasn't easy.

My chest hurt. My throat tingled.

My heart was pounding out of control.

And it was all because the last few hours wouldn't stop running through my head.

My brain was trying to reconcile it—the dinner, the conversation.

"*I want you back.*"

Jack's touch.

It wasn't just a simple swish of his fingers, a gentle clenching of my muscles and skin.

Nothing about Jack's hands was simple.

Because his touch wasn't just physical. It triggered emotions;

it induced memories. Ones that made me smile, ones that made me want to cry.

Having him back created a whole new set of challenges that was almost as scary as not having him here at all.

As I'd sat in his car, silence building between us, my hand on the seat belt and the other on the door, I'd wanted so badly to tell him what was on my mind. To say the words, so they'd stop eating at me.

But something stronger had consumed me, and that was the need to have his fingers on me again, to have his lips on mine without pushing them away.

And, now, I was hit with the aftermath, a whole new set of feelings.

Ones that were filling my eyes.

Ones that I wasn't even close to processing yet.

But I couldn't stay in here to do that, not with the elevator door sliding open to my floor.

So, I walked to my condo and put my key in the lock. Once I got inside, I immediately saw Anna in the living room, cuddled on the couch with a blanket over her.

The TV was on.

The scent of chocolate chip cookies was in the air, which I knew she'd made from scratch. They were Lucy's favorite, and Anna would do anything for her.

"How'd it go?" she asked.

I kicked off my heels and left them by the door.

"What's the face for?" She lifted the blanket, signaling me to come over and join her. "Are you crying?"

I hurried to the couch and snuggled into her side.

"Samantha, talk to me; you're starting to freak me out."

I used the blanket to wipe my cheeks. "I'm just having a minute."

She turned off the TV. "You're allowed to have as many as

you want, but you can't keep them a secret. Tell me what's going on in that little head of yours."

"Jack...obviously."

"Did something happen?"

I exhaled, the heaviness still very present in my chest. "He told me he wants me, and he apologized for the way he ended things. Then, we sorta hooked up in his car."

"You say that like it's a bad thing."

I sat up a little straighter, so I could look at her while I said, "Isn't it? I don't know. I've never been this confused in my life." I touched my chest, trying to ease it. "No, I take that back. I was this confused when Jack cut me off eight years ago." I leaned across the couch to the end table where I grabbed a tissue out of the box. "It's like he has a rope around me, and whenever he pulls, I turn into this crazy lunatic."

"I wouldn't call you crazy or a lunatic. I would say Jack's the man you're supposed to be with. He's your person, Samantha. And you're feeling this way because you care about him so much."

I gave her a side-eye.

"What? He is."

"I don't know."

"Are you really going to tell me you don't have feelings for him?"

I could still feel his hands on my body. My heart still hammered away at the thought of him, at the way his lips had pressed against mine. At the sound of him telling me he wanted me.

"No, I can't say that."

"I didn't think so."

"Even when I dated other men, I think Jack was always in the back of my mind."

"Girl, you're not telling me anything I don't already know."

She adjusted the blanket, so it covered more of me. "Where do things stand now?"

I balled the tissue in my hand and wiped the last drips from my eyes. "He wants to have dinner when he gets home from Nashville."

"Ah, what the hell is he doing there?"

"He's meeting with Shawn about work stuff, but he's also going to talk to Shawn about dating me."

"You're fucking kidding me."

I shook my head.

Anna got up from the couch and walked into the kitchen, grabbing a plate of cookies and setting them on the ottoman in front of us. She took two, handing me one and keeping the other for herself. "This is huge. You realize that, don't you?"

My stomach couldn't handle the idea of more food, so I put it back. "It brings things to a different level."

"And you're scared to death."

I wrapped my arms over the blanket. "I don't love the idea of Shawn and Jack talking about me, so that's one part of it. The other part is that I don't even know if I can trust Jack. What if I give him everything, and he leaves me again? I don't think I can handle going through that a second time." I tried to still the quivering that was happening inside my chest. "I want things to move slowly, and it feels like we're in fast-forward."

"Listen to me." As she shoved the rest of the cookie in her mouth, she pulled my hand into her lap and eventually surrounded it with both of hers. "This isn't something you can control. You just have to follow your gut and keep an open mind, and everything will fall into place."

"And stay guarded."

She squeezed my fingers. "And don't be guarded. If you face him with a shield, how do you expect him to find your heart?"

"You're too much right now, you hopeless romantic."

"Samantha"—her voice softened—"you're getting everything you ever wanted. Jack doesn't seem like the same man he once was. He sounds like he's grown into someone really amazing. Just take things one day at a time. If you do that, you'll be fine."

"God, this is so messy."

"It's really not." She rolled her eyes as though I were being the dramatic one. "It's just been two years since you've been with a man, so you're a little out of the game. I won't judge you for it."

"Anna, we both know my situation isn't typical." I tried to take a breath; the tightness was strangling me again. "That means nothing about a relationship with Jack will be typical."

"Ah, you mean the Lucy section of the equation. Do you think—"

I shook my head and cut her off with, "We're not talking about it."

"Samantha—"

"I can't go there yet."

I stood from the couch, dropping my tissue on the ottoman, and I moved toward the hallway.

"Where are you going?"

"To kiss Lucy good night. I'll be back in a minute."

I needed a break.

I needed silence.

I needed to keep that door closed for as long as I could.

Discussing it with Anna would only get me more worked up, and that was the last thing I needed right now.

I quietly tiptoed into Lucy's room and climbed onto her bed, lying in the small space next to her. With her back to me, I pressed my nose into her hair and inhaled the scent that was so unique to her.

My baby girl.

Every decision I made affected her, including whatever happened with Jack.

I closed my eyes and took a breath, trying to fight through these feelings. When I opened them again, I put my lips against Lucy's head. I felt the tears well up. I felt the tightening, the confusion, the worry, and the fear.

And then I whispered, "Oh God, baby. What have I done?"

Jack: I can still smell you.
Me: I thought you licked it all off.
Jack: I mean, your perfume. I can smell it on my suit. But I like where your head is, and yes, I did lick it all off.
Me: Naughty man.
Jack: Good night, gorgeous.

15

JACK

Me: *I'm headed to Nashville to meet with Shawn. I'm finally going to tell him the truth about Samantha.*
Brett: *Damn.*
Me: *I'm done hiding it. I like her, and her brother needs to fucking know.*
Brett: *That's my boy. Lay it all out there.*
Me: *I don't want him to think I'm choosing between the two of them. I can handle both as long as he can.*
Brett: *He won the Super Bowl. I don't think he has anything to complain about right now.*
Me: *Am I nuts to do this?*
Brett: *Any one of us would do the same. That's why we're best friends and business partners. We go after what we want. We don't fuck around.*
Me: *Let's hope he doesn't tackle me.*
Brett: *He's a tight end. What does he know about tackling?*
Me: *Good point.*

"JACK HUNT," Shawn said as he got closer to the table at a restaurant he'd told me to meet him at during my flight. He made his way around the booth, reaching down to clasp my hand and slap me on the shoulder. "It's good to see you, my man."

I could smell last night's booze on his breath. Not that I was surprised. I'd talked to him after I got back from having dinner with Samantha, and he was out drinking with his teammates. Hell, if I'd just won the Super Bowl, I'd have been doing the same. He'd worked hard for that championship, and he deserved to party his ass off.

"It's good to see you, too. You're doing all right?"

He sat down across from me. "Never better."

The waitress immediately came to our table, dropping off two coffees and two waters, both which I'd ordered before Shawn arrived. "I'm going to give you guys a minute to look at the menu," she said. "Can I get you anything in the meantime?"

I shook my head. Shawn did the same.

"Congrats on the win," she said before she walked away, wearing the biggest goddamn smile on her face.

"Are you getting a lot of attention?" I asked him once we were alone.

"You have no idea."

I didn't, and I was thankful for that. There were days when I wondered how Brett did it, constantly getting his picture taken whenever he was with James in LA. That was a life I didn't want.

He nodded toward the folder that I'd placed next to me on the table. "You've got some good numbers for me?"

My assistant had printed out every offer that had come in over the last few days, and I'd reviewed each one along with the terms of the contract, so I could explain them in detail.

He had some serious decisions to make.

Ones that would financially set him up for the rest of his life.

But, before we talked money, I had to get this thing with

Samantha off my chest. This conversation had been weighing on me the whole fight here, and I didn't want to wait any longer.

"There's something I need to talk to you about first," I said.

I wasn't a nervous person. I went into business meetings confident as hell because I knew the industry backward and forward, and I dared anyone to challenge me. I had a law degree, and I considered myself an expert negotiator.

But, as I looked into the face of one of my very first clients, I wasn't feeling so sure of myself.

This was personal.

This was his fucking sister.

He lifted his coffee and took a sip. "Your walking papers had better not be in that folder because there's no way I'm letting you quit."

I wondered if he'd still say that once I told him what was on my mind.

"I'm not going anywhere."

"Then, what's going on?"

I left the coffee alone, but I filled my mouth with water, and then I cleared my throat. "We need to chat about Samantha."

"Samantha?" His brows rose. "You mean, my sister? What about her? Is she in trouble or something?"

"We've been talking."

He laughed, and that surprised the hell out of me. "If you're thinking about making her into an athlete, you're going after the wrong sister. Samantha didn't play any sports in school. The girl has no aim and even less coordination. Stacey is the only other athlete in my family. She got a golfing scholarship, and she could have gone pro, had she wanted it badly enough."

Jesus Christ.

"Shawn, I don't want to represent your sister. I want to date her."

As the seconds passed, it looked like my words were finally starting to sink in.

"Oh, shit." He continued to stare at me. "You want to date my sister."

"I'd like to, yeah."

"Have you spent a lot of time with her?"

I couldn't get a read on him. He wasn't acting pissed, but he wasn't acting pleased either.

"Yes," I answered.

"How long have you guys been talking?"

"Not long."

That wasn't a lie since we hadn't really done much talking eight years ago.

Not that I'd ever mention any of that shit to him.

"I respect you, Shawn. So, before things go any further between Samantha and me, I wanted to discuss it with you."

It looked like he was still processing the news, still unsure of how he felt about it. "I like that you came to me, and I appreciate it."

I wanted him to know that Samantha wasn't just someone I'd talked to at the bar and decided I wanted to hang out with. I was coming to him because I wanted to take things to a deeper level.

"Shawn, your sister is a hell of a girl. She's patient and sweet; she's understanding and forgiving. She works as much as I do, and you know how important that is, given how often I travel."

"I know."

"What I'm trying to say is, I care about her. Enough that I'm coming to you, my client and my friend, and I'm putting our professional relationship on the line because your sister's worth it."

His lids narrowed, his stare intensifying. "All right, I can see it now."

"You can?"

"Yeah, man. It took me a second, which is probably due to all the shit I drank last night, but yes, I can see the two of you together. She's a great girl; you're a nice guy. You both live in Miami. The fit makes sense."

Motherfucker.

All that buildup for nothing.

"I want her to be happy," he said. "So, I've got no problem with it."

I shook my head, sighing, relieved that we'd made it through that conversation.

"But, Jack, I'm going to warn you about something right now."

I'd thought I was in the clear.

Sounded like I'd thought wrong.

"If you hurt Samantha or Lucy, you'll have to answer to me."

Lucy?

I stared at him, waiting for an explanation to follow. When one didn't come, I said, "Who's Lucy?"

"Who's Lucy?" He laughed much harder this time. "You're serious?"

"Yeah, I'm serious. Who is she?"

"Lucy is Samantha's daughter."

Samantha's daughter?

No way.

It wasn't even fucking possible.

I'd heard him wrong.

"What did you say?" I asked.

He leaned his elbows on the table. "Lucy's her baby girl and my niece." As he stared at me, his expression began to change. "Shit, she didn't tell you."

I couldn't believe he was talking about the same fucking woman I had fingered in my car last night. About the woman I had texted before I went to bed. About the woman I hadn't been able to get out of my mind since I saw her at his Super Bowl.

I shook my head.

"I didn't mean to be the one to break the news," he said. "I'm shocked she didn't tell you. That little girl is her whole world."

I tried to calm my voice, masking the anger that wanted to come through. "I'm sure she is. What about the dad? Is he still in the picture?"

Shawn shook his head. "Nah."

I didn't even know what the fuck to say.

I didn't understand why Samantha hadn't told me or why she was keeping her daughter a secret.

Or if this news was going to change the possibility of us having a future.

"My niece is a massive part of my life," he said. "I'd do anything for either of those girls, and I'm extremely protective of them. So, you'd better be good to them, Jack."

I looked at the mug of coffee and at the half-empty glass of water, wishing like hell they were full of something stronger.

And then I finally glanced at him. "I hear your message, Shawn. Loud and clear."

Me: She has a fucking kid.
Brett: Who?
Me: Samantha.
Brett: She just told you that?
Me: No, her fucking brother told me. Samantha hasn't said a goddamn word about it.
Brett: Jesus. There must be a reason she didn't tell you.
Me: Whatever her reasoning is, it's bullshit.
Brett: Go pour yourself a drink.

Me: And then what?
Brett: And then don't call her because that's a conversation you should have with her in person.

I left the hotel bar and stumbled up to my room. I'd spent the last few hours there, drinking scotch and watching the Rangers destroy the Bruins. I represented New York's starting right wing, and during the second period, he had been taken in the locker room for a lower body injury. I'd already put a call in to the team doctor, both trainers, and the player's wife. I didn't expect to hear anything until after they got the results of the X-rays, which would be within the hour.

I wouldn't have a problem with staying up to wait for that call.

Sleep wasn't going to come anytime soon.

Not when the thought of Samantha and her little girl was running through my head like a fucking song on repeat.

When I got inside my suite, I stripped out of my suit and hung it across one of the chairs. I climbed into bed, staring at my phone.

Brett had told me not to call her. He'd told me not to bring up the kid until I got back to Miami.

It was good advice.

Especially because I was in no condition to have that conversation right now. Not after how much scotch I'd shot back at the bar.

Still, Samantha knew I was in Nashville, she knew I was meeting with her brother today, and she knew I was going to mention something to him. It would be fucked up if I didn't at least reach out.

So, I opened her last text, and I began to type.

Me: I'm in bed.
Samantha: Me, too.
Me: Long day?
Samantha: It was a busy one. You?
Me: Yeah, you could say that.
Samantha: Is everything all right?
Me: Scotch. Lots of it. I'm about to fall asleep.
Samantha: Good night, Jack.

My thumbs hovered over the screen as I stared at her words.
I touched a letter on my keyboard and a second one.
But I couldn't do it.
I couldn't say anything.
I had to listen to Brett.
I deleted what I had typed and put my phone on the night-stand, replacing it with the remote, my thumb tapping the button that changed the channel.
That button was safer.
That button I wouldn't regret pushing in the morning.

16

SAMANTHA

THE RINGING of my cell woke me up, so I reached across my nightstand, feeling all around the wood until my fingers hit my phone. Gripping it in my hand, I checked the screen to see who was calling and brought it up to my ear. "Shawn, is everything okay?"

"Sam," he said as music blasted in the background, several other voices shouting nearby.

I took a quick glance at the screen again to see what time it was. It was just after one in the morning. He must be at a bar.

"I have to tell you something," he said in a voice that told me he was drunk.

"What's wrong?"

"I told him."

I shot up in bed, my back pushing against the headboard as I tried to work through the grogginess. "Who? And what did you tell?"

As he sighed, the music and the voices turned softer, which meant he was moving into a different room. "I only wanted to give a warning, you know? 'Cause I love you and Lucy, and I want to protect you."

I flipped on the lamp that was beside my bed and pulled the blanket up to my chin, tucking my knees against my chest. "Shawn, what are you saying?"

"Jack and I met up, and we talked about you."

"I know; he told me he was going to say something to you. Did something happen?"

Although part of me had found it adorable that Jack wanted to have a chat with Shawn, I was terrified at the same time. The last thing I wanted was for Shawn to tell Jack about my daughter. I'd considered telling Shawn not to say anything about her. But asking him to hide her was almost like asking him to lie. I couldn't do that to Shawn. More importantly, I couldn't do that to my daughter.

"Fuck, Sam." He paused. Even through his buzz, I could hear his emotions, and they made me more nervous. "I told him that, if he hurt you or Lucy, he'd have to answer to me."

"Oh God," I whispered.

I almost dropped the phone; my heart was thumping so hard.

My biggest fear had come true because I was positive Jack had then asked who Lucy was.

This was my fault, not Shawn's.

I couldn't even be mad at my brother.

I'd put him in this situation.

I'd put all of us in this situation.

But, still, it should have been me who told Jack.

It should have been me who slowly broke the news, not thrown it on him in a roundabout way that probably confused and angered and shocked him to death.

"Jack's reaction told me he didn't know anything about her." He let out a huge breath. "Christ, Sam, I had no idea he didn't know."

"I know. It's okay."

It wasn't.

And I didn't know if it would be, but I couldn't make Shawn feel bad about this.

"It took balls for him to come to me, so he must like you, and you must like him. So, why were you keeping Lucy a secret?"

"I don't know." That wasn't the truth. "I was waiting for the right time to tell him, I guess."

There was no right time.

I would have waited until I had no other choice.

Until I couldn't put it off a second longer.

Because I was worried about what he would think.

I was worried he wouldn't be interested in me anymore.

My worries didn't even end there.

"I'm sorry, Sam."

"It's okay. But I have to go. I'll call you tomorrow."

I didn't say good-bye, nor did I wait for him to say it before I hung up and put the phone on my lap.

I couldn't call Jack right now.

It certainly didn't feel right to text him.

I'd just have to wait until he returned to Miami, which wouldn't be for another night, and then I'd explain it all to him then.

Remembering our text exchange from earlier, I clicked on the Messages app and opened our conversation, reading everything he had typed.

Something had felt off. At the time, I hadn't thought much of it.

But, now, I knew why.

17

JACK

IT HAD BEEN a long few days in Nashville. After spending the first night in my hotel room alone, I'd decided to go out with Shawn the following evening, and we partied until three that morning. Five hours later, I'd hopped on our company jet and flown back to Miami where I spent the rest of the day working on the contracts Shawn had chosen. I changed the terms of every agreement, and I asked for more money than had originally been offered. Now, I was just waiting to hear if they accepted or if they wanted to keep negotiating.

I was fucking exhausted by the time I closed the last folder and cleared off my desk.

Knowing I had to meet Samantha for dinner in less than an hour, I pulled out my phone and began to type her a text.

Me: Would you mind eating at my place instead of going out?
Samantha: That's fine.
Me: I'll get something delivered.
Samantha: No, don't worry about it. I'll bring the food.
Me: I live in The Towers. It's four buildings down from yours,

same side of the street, toward the causeway. I'm in the penthouse.
See you at 7.

I left the office and went straight to my place, grabbing a beer from the fridge before I made my way into my bedroom. Once inside, I stripped out of my suit and brought the beer into the shower, setting it on the shampoo shelf. I turned the temperature as hot as I could stand it, put my arms above my head, and pressed my palms against the tiles. Streams of scalding water shot out of the ceiling and two of the walls, hitting me at every angle.

As my skin became drenched, I thought about Samantha.

Before I had known she had a kid, I had no problem visualizing my life with her. Now that I knew she was responsible for someone else, someone who would always come first, that changed things.

She should have fucking told me.

In fact, it should have been one of the first things she said, so I knew what I was getting involved in.

Whether I liked it or not, I was in neck deep with a girl who was already a mother, and that was a heavier situation than I'd ever been in.

I took the beer off the shelf and guzzled half of it. It tasted good. It felt even better, the freezing brew drizzling down my throat, the only part of my body that wasn't being pounded with something that was scorching.

But it did nothing to help the thoughts, to give me any clarity, to justify Samantha's actions.

I set the beer back, and I squirted some soap into my hands, rubbing my fingers over me, working up a thick lather. When my flesh was covered in suds, I shampooed my hair and beard. Then, I put my hands back on the wall, and I let the water wash it all away.

Once I finished, I grabbed the bottle, wrapped a towel around my waist, and moved over to the sink. I quickly rolled on some deodorant, sprayed cologne on my neck, and dressed in a pair of sweats and a T-shirt.

By the time I walked out of my room, a ringing sound was coming through the tablet by the elevator, alerting me that the front desk was trying to reach me. I went over to the tablet and pressed the screen.

A picture of the doorman came into view. "Mr. Hunt, Samantha Cole is here to see you. Her identification has been checked, and she's been processed into our system."

"Send her up."

Moving back into the kitchen, I grabbed another beer from the fridge, twisted off the cap, and tossed the metal into the trash. I was holding the bottle up to my lips when I heard the sound of the elevator opening directly into my condo. Footsteps followed. And, within a few seconds, Samantha was rounding the corner, holding two large bags from the sushi restaurant down the block.

"Since we were going for sushi, I figured you must like it. I just didn't know what kinds you preferred, so I ordered a little bit of everything." She set the bags on the island and came over to me, her hands falling against the tops of my shoulders. "Hi."

I softly kissed her. "Thanks for bringing the food."

She nodded.

I felt a change.

A distance.

That told me she'd had a conversation with Shawn. She knew that I knew about her daughter. Therefore, she knew, tonight, we were going to talk.

With her hands still on me, she took a quick look around the kitchen. "I like your taste. Whoever decorated did a wonderful job."

"It wasn't me."

"I figured."

She stood on her toes to reach my cheek, which she gently kissed, and I did the same to hers. And then she went to the island and reached into one of the bags.

From where I stood, I was able to see all of her, and I held the beer to my mouth and swallowed as my eyes drifted down her body. She was casual tonight in a pair of tight jeans and a tank top that she'd tied in the middle, so it now showed a sliver of her stomach. The pants she had on outlined those perfect hips and the gap between those toned thighs.

I wanted to fucking growl as I took her in.

But a conversation needed to be had first, and I didn't know what that was going to do to us.

She took out the multiple containers that each held a different roll, and she opened them and spread them over the counter. As she finished, she put a pair of chopsticks, a large bowl of soy sauce, and chunks of wasabi and ginger in front of me.

She hadn't forgotten anything.

The same way a mother wouldn't.

Fuck.

"Do you want anything to drink?" I asked.

She nodded toward my beer. "I'll have the same."

When I returned from the fridge, she'd put a barstool across from hers, so we could face each other on opposite sides of the island. She'd also placed two small plates in each spot, moving the chopsticks right next to them.

More motherly shit.

I took a seat and opened the wooden sticks, looking at all the rolls. The first one I picked was covered in avocado. I dipped it in soy sauce before I popped it into my mouth. It was good as hell. So were the next two and the lump of ginger I took in.

"Jack..."

I looked up from my plate, and that was when I realized she hadn't even opened her chopsticks. "Yeah?"

I knew what was coming.

I just needed a little food in me first because I'd been too busy to eat all day.

"I know my brother told you about Lucy. I can't sit here for another second and wait for you to bring it up. I need to talk to you about it before I explode."

I freed my hands and rested my elbows on the counter, using my palms to hold my chin. "Go ahead and talk. I'm listening."

"Are you angry with me?"

It took me a second to answer. "I'm not angry that you have a child. I'm angry you didn't tell me about her and that you weren't comfortable enough to share something like that with me." There was so much emotion in her face, in the way she was breathing, how she had her arms wrapped around her, and I knew this conversation wasn't easy for her to have. "We went through an entire dinner where we talked about what'd been happening in our lives, and you said nothing about her." I sighed, shaking my head. "And then I went on to apologize for how I'd treated you, I told you I wanted you back, and you still said nothing. I'm having a hard time understanding why you hid her from me."

"It was wrong; I should have told you. I..." Shawn had said that Samantha's daughter was her whole world. Now that the topic was on her, I could see that in her eyes. "I had no idea what was happening between us. You came into my life so quickly, and suddenly, I was seeing you and thinking about you and spending time with you. You have to understand, I'm extremely protective of her. I know it wasn't right, but until I knew what was really happening between us, I didn't want to bring her into it."

"But she's a part of you. I can't decide to be with one without knowing about the other."

"I know." Her voice was so quiet. "It was wrong of me. That's all I can say."

"I went to your goddamn brother to talk to him about you, so you had to know I was serious."

When her arms tightened around her, they pushed her tits closer together. "It's been a long time since I've had any feelings for someone, and the last few days have been a lot to process." She started to rock a little over the stool. "I didn't expect this. I wasn't prepared. And I didn't handle it in the best way. I'm sorry, Jack. I really am." Her eyes dropped to the plate in front of me. "I'm just trying to do the best I can."

"She obviously changes things."

Her eyes shot back up. "How?"

I almost laughed. "How? I can't just come to your place whenever I want. I can't steal you away for a weekend. I can't get you to stay here for nights at a time. Our evenings together will have to be scheduled, so you can find someone to watch her." I took a drink of my beer. "You're a single mother; your daughter will always come first. I don't want to be the dick who asks you to make me a priority, especially because it sounds like it's just the two of you and her dad isn't in the picture."

Her eyes widened, and she paused for several seconds. I could tell she was fighting with her emotions. I could tell that even more when she got up from the island and threw something in the trash like she just needed a break from our conversation.

"He's not," she finally said when she turned back toward me, returning to her stool, her chest rising and falling so fucking fast. "But none of that changes how I feel about you. Can you say the same?"

I'd thought about that question from the moment I left the restaurant with Shawn.

Her daughter didn't change my feelings, but she changed things between Samantha and me. Our relationship would be different than what I'd expected it to be.

Knowing I couldn't spend as much time with her as I wanted was disappointing.

Knowing I wouldn't come first was, too, and that was something I'd have to get used to.

"No," I finally said. "It doesn't change the way I feel about you."

She set her hands on the counter, and I saw how white they were from how tightly she'd been squeezing them around her. "I want us to have a chance."

"Have you really thought about that? What it would look like?"

She nodded, following that with, "Yes."

She'd apologized.

She cared about me.

And something told me she'd try to find a balance.

"You want this?" My feet pushed against the ground, my elbows driving into the countertop. "Are you sure?"

"Yes, Jack. You're what I want. There isn't a question in my mind."

I stood and walked over to her. When she didn't look at me right away, I put my fingers under her chin and tilted her head back until our eyes met. "I need to know you're not going to hide things from me. That when we're faced with something tough, you're going to be willing to talk through it."

She took a breath. "Jack..."

"Because if this is what you want, if I'm what you want, then we'll find a way to make this work."

"I do." She chewed the corner of her lip, her eyes pleading with mine. "I really do."

"Listen, I've never dated anyone who has a child. I don't know the rules or the boundaries, but I'll learn, and we'll figure it out together."

"That's all I want."

She seemed to be relieved, but I could still see so much turmoil in her. The only way I knew how to make her feel better was to wrap my arms around her waist and pull her against my chest. So, I did, and I kissed the top of her head. I breathed her in until her face moved out of my T-shirt, and she gazed up at me. Her lips looked so soft and smooth. I leaned down and rubbed my bottom lip over them.

The scent of cinnamon had made it all the way into her mouth, tasting so good, I wanted to lick it off her. But, before I did that, I needed to know she was okay with the conversation we'd just had. And the only way I could do that was by making her come to me.

I held the sides of her face and said, "Kiss me."

After a few seconds, she pushed her mouth on mine, and I felt her relax a little. I took in the small amount of tongue she had given me, circling around it.

Her hands went to my chest, her nails scraping my flesh during the climb. When she reached the top of my T-shirt, I felt her grip it as though she wanted to pull it over my head.

I broke our kiss, sliding back a few inches to look at her. "Fuck, I want you."

"Jack, don't make me wait."

"Samantha—"

"I want more than just your fingers tonight."

I gripped her harder, lifting her off the stool and wrapping her legs around me. "Kiss me," I demanded again, and I carried her to my bedroom.

When I set her on the bed, I broke our kiss to take off her tank top and do the same with her shoes and jeans. Now, she was only in a pair of red panties and a matching bra.

Goddamn it.

She was fucking gorgeous. Exactly the way I remembered,

but her body was tighter, her skin a little tanner, her curves even sexier.

"You're perfect."

"Come here," she said, reaching for me from between her legs.

She gripped the waist of my sweats and let them drop to the floor, doing the same with my T-shirt, and now, I was standing in front of her in just my boxer briefs.

I knelt on the bed, my lips pressing on the middle of her stomach, and I kissed across her navel, up to her bra, and back down to lick the top of her panties.

More cinnamon.

More lace.

They reminded me of the first pair I'd ripped off of her eight years ago.

Slowly, I yanked them down her legs, my mouth diving straight to her pussy. I grazed over her clit, my tongue spreading the wetness, the tip of it flicking across the very top of her, which I knew was one of her most sensitive places.

She grasped my hair and twisted it around her fingers. "Jack, don't stop."

I groaned in response, my fucking cock so hard, it was grinding into the bed. I reached down and gave it a few pumps, the need to be inside her causing me to lick even faster.

"You taste so goddamn good."

I lowered a few inches, my nose pressed into her lips, and I inhaled.

That fucking scent.

I wanted it to be the first thing I smelled every morning when I woke up, her pussy the first thing that touched my tongue long before I even brushed my teeth.

I inserted two fingers, and she immediately started to ride

them. It was the hottest sight to see them buried deep within her, her clit so wet from my tongue.

Pleasure spread across her face. "Jack," she breathed.

She didn't have to tell me. Her pussy was clenching me so hard, it was as though my cock were inside her, and she was trying to milk the cum out of it. But then she tightened even more, her stomach shuddering, and I knew she'd hit her peak. So, I pointed my tongue at the top of that hard bud, and I licked it as hard and as fast as I could.

Her hips bucked, her breath released in short screams, and her body quivered.

When she finally stilled, I pulled out of her, and I moved her higher on the bed.

I didn't join her right away. I walked over to the nightstand first to grab a condom and I let my boxer briefs fall to the ground while I rolled it onto my cock. Then, I climbed over her body.

"I forgot how good your tongue was," she said.

I wiped my hand over my beard, drying all the wetness before I pressed my lips against hers. "If I didn't want to fuck you so badly, I'd remind you all night."

"My God, you're incredible."

I moved in between her thighs, and while I kept them spread, I aimed my dick at her entrance. Her pussy was so wet, I knew I didn't need to add any more to it, so I gently tilted my hips and drove in a few inches, letting her get used to what I felt like again.

Her head leaned back, and her mouth opened. "More."

Slowly, I continued to bury myself until she had all of me. "Fuck," I hissed, pausing to let her loosen, feeling her muscles constrict around my cock.

She was still so fucking tight.

So wet.

So goddamn warm.

When her stare connected with mine, I lifted her back off the bed, and I pushed her higher until it hit the headboard. Then, I gripped the top of the wood and used it to rock my hips forward.

"*Ahhh!*" she yelled.

I gave her another thrust, and the same noise shot out of her.

"Too much?"

"No." She gnawed into her lip. "Don't you dare stop."

That was the answer I wanted.

I stroked in and out, easily finding a rhythm, pushing my way through her tightness.

She felt so fucking good.

"Hold on to me, baby," I told her once I felt her cunt start to contract.

Her hands slid to my back, her nails pressing into my skin. She could dig all she wanted. The only thing it did was show me how much she liked it, and that turned me on even more.

She groaned so loudly. "You're going to make me come again."

She barely had the words out before I felt her get wetter, her clenching causing my own orgasm to work its way through my balls.

I reared my hips back and pounded into her.

"Jack!"

"Say it fucking louder."

When she did, I looked down and ordered her to, "Kiss me."

I was met with her lips and a moan that I could taste on my tongue.

When I knew she was lost in sensations, her body trembling through each wave, I emptied myself inside her.

Finally catching my breath, I pulled away from her mouth and wrapped myself around her body. "You feel so good."

She nuzzled her face into my neck. "I've missed you. No one makes me feel the way you do."

I fucking loved hearing that.

I especially liked knowing that no one but me could give her body what she wanted. I knew most of her spots, the ones she liked touched and the ones she preferred to have licked. I planned on learning the rest very soon.

Possibly even later this evening, which got me thinking. "Do you have to go home tonight?"

"No."

"Good." I grazed my nose across the side of her hair. "I need to toss this condom, and then we have some sushi to eat."

"God, I forgot all about the food."

I kissed her cheek and the tip of her nose and the center of her forehead. "You need to eat."

She let out a light laugh. "Why?"

"Because you're going to need fuel for what I plan on doing to you all night."

"You're just as naughty as you were eight years ago."

"Oh no, Samantha." I bit down on her bottom lip, tugging it between mine. "I'm much worse now."

18

SAMANTHA

WHEN I RAN up to the entrance of Anna's building, I was immediately greeted by her doorman, who smiled and said, "Good morning, Miss Cole. It's nice to see you."

"Morning," I replied, completely out of breath.

I rushed into the lobby and went over to the elevator where I slammed my finger on the button, hoping it would open quickly.

"Do you want me to call Miss Shay and let her know you're here?"

The elevator arrived, and I stepped inside, pressing the button for Anna's floor. "No, I'm sure she is asleep and won't answer." I rested my hand on my chest, trying to calm the anxiety surrounding my heart.

"Have a good day," he said.

I waved as the door closed. Then, I used the same hand to grip the safety bar behind me, needing it to bear some of my weight.

The heaviness of my body was becoming too much.

I was grateful Anna worked nights and was always home in the morning. The short window between dropping Lucy off and my first meeting was the only time I ever had available to come here. I was even more grateful of that today because I needed my best friend.

The elevator stopped on her floor, and I used the set of keys she'd given me to open her door. I darted past the kitchen and went right to the guest room where I always checked for her first. Even though she kept her nursing license active, Anna now worked as a fetish model where she was paid to show her feet on a live cam. Often pulling all-nighters, she would sometimes be filming when I arrived. Fortunately, that wasn't the case now. The lights had been turned off, the props had been put away, and the red light was missing from the camera.

Had she been in the middle of a scene, it could have been hours before she was able to talk.

That was another thing I was grateful for this morning.

I continued down the hallway and slipped inside her room, taking a seat on the other side of the mattress. My hand fell against her arm, and I shook it to wake her.

She groaned and pulled the blanket over her head. "I worked until five this morning—which was, what? An hour ago I'm guessing? So, unless you are hot, single, and have the most glorious penis in Miami, or you have a coffee that's a minimum of sixty ounces, let me sleep."

"Anna," I whispered.

"Oh, fuck." She tossed the blanket off and immediately faced me. "You sound like shit. What happened?"

Now that I was here, sitting so close to her, the memories from the last hour started screaming inside my head again.

"Does she have your eyes?" Jack asked as his mouth left mine.
"Who?"

"Lucy."

"No, she has her father's eyes."

I couldn't breathe.

It felt like a pair of hands were around my throat, squeezing all the air out of me, and there were feet stomping on my chest, putting too much pressure on my heart.

"Samantha." She grasped my shoulders, observing my face, scanning my eyes, as she looked at me like I was a patient. "What's going on? You're worrying me."

I shook my head, trying to force out my thoughts. "I want him, and I want him to be in our lives."

"Pause for a second." She got up from the bed, went into the bathroom, and returned with a box of tissues. She took several in her hand and blotted them against my face, catching tears that I hadn't realized had fallen. "You've made a decision. Finally. That's a good thing, babe."

"No."

I tried to swallow, but the spit wouldn't go down. My throat was too constricted. My breathing was becoming shallow, air barely passing through.

"Why are you so upset?"

I shook my head again, trying to reach for the thoughts, but when I opened my mouth, they wouldn't come out. A sob burst through instead, and I felt myself panting, and my skin turned flushed, clamminess covering me.

"Samantha, you need to take a few deep breaths, or you're going to pass out."

This was the nurse in her.

But, this time, unlike so many others, it wouldn't heal me.

Nothing could.

Her hands moved back to my shoulders, and she squeezed. "Big breaths."

"I can't," I huffed.

Her fingers went to my chin, and she held my face, so I was forced to look at her. "You have to. Breathe in through your nose and out through your mouth. Focus, Samantha; it'll make you feel better."

"No," I cried.

It wouldn't. I was so sure of that.

But I still tried to follow her instructions, bypassing the tightness and making the thoughts stop spinning for just a second. When I did, things started to loosen.

"That's it," she encouraged. "Just a few more deep breaths, and the panic attack will pass."

It had been years since I had one.

Eight years to be exact.

The last one had felt just like this.

Ironically, they were over the same person.

"I fucked up so badly," I said once I was able to take in enough air.

"Honey, how?" She put a tissue in my hand and held another against my face to dry my cheeks. "I'm sure it's not as bad as you think."

I looked down, the shame tearing me apart. "You know I went over to Jack's last night to talk to him about Lucy?"

"Yes. I know."

"Well, we discussed her." I paused, the tightness returning. I tried swallowing it down, and all it did was get worse. "Anna"—I finally looked up at her again—"I couldn't tell him. I had the perfect opportunity, and I wanted to so badly. The words were there; they were on my tongue, I just couldn't say them out loud. I was just so scared." The strangling returned, and so did the feeling of someone stepping on my chest. "He asked me this morning if Lucy had my eyes, and I couldn't get out of his condo fast enough. I told him I had a meeting, and I rushed downstairs. I held on to my bag, and I ran all five blocks to your building." My body started to rock back and forth. "What have I done? How the hell am I going to fix this?"

"Oh God."

"He asked about her father. I told him he wasn't in the picture anymore and..."

"You lied."

Tears fell from my chin as I nodded. "He's never going to forgive me this time. I had a chance to come clean, to make this right, to tell him the truth. And I blew it."

"Samantha—"

"How do I tell him, Anna? How do I look him in the face and say, *You're Lucy's father?*"

She grabbed another handful of tissues, but I didn't want them. I placed them on the mattress and let the tears soak in, let the spit fly from my lips, let the snot run from my nose.

The guilt of never telling Jack about his daughter had been eating me alive for eight years. I knew, no matter what I said to him or Lucy, keeping this secret was the most selfish act a mother could commit. No amount of tissues or deep breathing could take away my deceit. I could only hope that, one day, they would both forgive me.

"She's seven years old," I said in a hoarse voice, my throat so restricted. "She's never met her father. She only knows the fairy-tale image that I've painted of him. When I got pregnant, I thought I was doing what he wanted, and that was staying away from him. But I've lived with this regret for too long. I can't do it anymore."

"You should have told him." Her tone forced my eyes to lock with hers.

She was always on my side, always had my back.

But not now.

I saw the disappointment on her face, and that hurt so much.

Yet I deserved it. Every bit of it.

"You're absolutely right. I should have told him," I said.

"Now, you have to go do it. Because that man needs to know that gorgeous little girl is his."

The tightening clenched even harder.

My chest felt like it was going to explode.

My entire body shook.

And it got even worse as I pictured my daughter in my head.

She was so beautiful.

She had her father's stunning, big blue eyes. His smile. His charm. His wit.

I had to tell him.

And then, somehow, I had to tell Lucy.

I found my purse on the floor. I didn't even remember dropping it before I had crawled into her bed. I dug around inside until I found my phone. "I'm going to ask if I can see him tonight."

"Who's going to watch Lucy?"

"My parents."

Me: Can I see you again tonight? Your place? Dinner?

I set the phone on her bed, and another thought hit me. This one hurt as much as the others. "Oh my God, I'm going to have to tell my family, too. What are they going to think when they find out that Jack is Lucy's father?"

Everyone thought her father was a boy from the University of Miami. A one-night stand whose name I never knew. But, to Lucy, I had described her father in a much different way. She knew more than anyone else.

"Let's just take this one day at a time because this isn't going to be pretty. At all," she said. "But you have to do it. You can't put it off any longer."

My world had changed the night of the NFL draft.

It had changed again the night of the Super Bowl.

And it would change once more tonight.

"You're going to be all right, no matter what," she said. Her hand was on mine, our fingers linked, my tear-soaked skin dampening hers. "We survived your pregnancy, Lucy's birth, and seven years of her life. We'll get through this, too."

I nodded, but I said nothing.

I couldn't.

19

JACK

Me: Two nights in a row? Fuck, you must have read my mind.
Samantha: Nope, I just need to see you.
Me: Damn it, I need to see you. You rushed out of my place so fast
this morning; I didn't get a chance to taste you again like I wanted.
New rule...
Samantha: Rule?
Me: You don't get out of my bed in the morning until I've tasted
you at least twice. No exceptions. I'm going to prove that even
more tonight. Have yourself a good day, Samantha. I'll see
you later.

"DO you want to talk about it?" Brett asked as he stood in the doorway of my office.

I hadn't realized he was there, so I set my phone on top of my desk and said, "Come on in."

"I take it, you and Samantha talked?"

I shrugged. "She apologized for not telling me about her

daughter, and we're going to try to figure this shit out. Man, I don't have a fucking clue how to navigate this one, but I guess it'll make sense over time."

He took a seat in one of the chairs in front of me. "The first step was her brother, and you made it through that. Now, I'm sure she has to figure out how to balance you and the little girl. Is the dad still in the picture?"

"No, it doesn't sound like he ever was."

Brett lifted a squish ball off my desk and tossed it into the air, caught it, and threw it high again. "Are you going to meet her kid right away?"

"She didn't bring that up, but I have a feeling, it's going to take a while."

"That's probably for the better. You can get you two figured out and then see how the little one fits in." He set the ball down and grabbed one of the folders that held Shawn's contracts. "Is Puma in here?"

I nodded. "Man, you weren't fucking kidding. They're playing hardball."

"How about the others?"

"I should have the final numbers worked out within a few weeks. The contracts are going back and forth between the lawyers now that I've negotiated all the terms. You know, those greedy bastards have to weigh in and take their cut, too."

"Says the dude with a law degree."

I laughed at how true that statement was. "What do you have going on today?"

"I'm flying out tomorrow to go to Atlanta and then swinging by Memphis, Detroit, and Vegas where I've got clients shooting. My last stop will be LA where I'll see James for a few days, and then I'll come back to Miami. I think I'm going to head out of here after lunch and take the afternoon off."

"Max is about to go on the road, too."

I'd checked his schedule this morning before I stopped by his office to talk to him. I hadn't seen much of him in the last few weeks, and I missed that fucker.

Brett picked up the ball again and tossed it to me. "I'm going to see him in LA while he's out there, visiting Eve."

I tossed the ball back to him just as a celebrity alert came across my phone. Several would come in a day, broadcasting whatever piece of gossip to millions of subscribers.

Just in case they involved one of my clients, I read every one that flashed across my screen.

This time, it was about someone I represented.

And it was also about our best friend.

BREAKING NEWS
SCARLETT DAVIS, MIAMI'S MOST DESIRED BACHELORETTE, WAS SEEN OUT LAST NIGHT WITH VINCE HEDMAN. SORRY, GUYS, IT LOOKS LIKE THE FIERY CFO HAS HOOKED HERSELF A DOLPHIN.

"You're fucking kidding me," I said, reading the headline several times before I clicked on the photos.

There were three. Two showed Vince and Scarlett holding hands as they walked in South Beach. The third was a shot of them kissing.

"Look at this shit." I held the phone, so Brett could see the screen.

"Jesus Christ."

"Did you know about this?"

"Fuck no."

I got up from my desk. "I'm getting to the bottom of it right now."

I went down the short hallway until I reached Scarlett's office. Her door was closed, but I could hear her on the phone. I stood there for a few seconds, and when she still hadn't hung up, I knocked. Not waiting for a response, I went in, and she watched us walk toward her, the two of us sitting in front of her desk.

"Tell him I'm fucking pissed," she barked into the phone. "Tell him I want his balls on a fucking stake, and that whoever took those goddamn photos was invading my privacy. You'll be hearing from my attorney." She slammed down the phone, took a breath, and smiled.

She was as ruthless as her three partners.

"Vince Hedman, huh?" I said.

"Oh God." She rolled her eyes and crossed her arms over her chest. "Not you, too."

"Were you going to tell us?" I asked.

"Were you going to tell me you were fucking Samantha Cole?" she came back with.

Brett laughed so goddamn hard.

So did I. "Touché, my friend." I looked at Brett. "What the hell is going on at The Agency? You're engaged to your own client." I glanced at Scarlett. "You're dating my quarterback. Who the fuck is next?"

"You and Max are off the market, so I think we're good for a little while," Brett said. "Scarlett, when did you start talking to Vince?"

"The night of the Super Bowl." She smiled and nodded toward me. "I know it was the same night for you and Samantha. But you might want to fill Max in before he reads it in a celebrity alert and gets pissy, like the two of you just were."

"There won't be one," I assured her. "No one gives a fuck about me, and Samantha isn't a celebrity."

"No one gives a fuck?" Scarlett mocked. "Have you forgotten about all the women who have tried to tame you over the years? The athletes, singers, and the actresses? When news gets out that you're a taken man, I'd say a whole lot of bitches are going to care."

My eyes shifted over to Brett. "Is she serious?"

He put his hands in the air. "Fuck if I know. I'm just glad it wasn't my name in the alert this time. I've had way too many of those written about me."

I shook my head. "I thought we promised no drama at The Agency?"

The two of them laughed.

"We signed twenty-two new clients today," Scarlett said. "We've brought in over sixty million this month, and we have over two hundred agents applying to work here every week. I say we keep the alerts coming. It's definitely good for business."

20

SAMANTHA

"WE'RE ONLY GOING to be here for a few minutes," I said to Lucy as the doorman escorted us to James's private elevator. "Then, we'll go and get some ice cream and then pedicures." Lucy and I stepped inside the small space, and I thanked him before the door closed, the elevator immediately taking off for the penthouse.

"I really want cookie dough ice cream," she squealed.

"I want strawberry." I gently dragged my fingers through the front of her hair, her strands long and dark like mine. "I'll be super quick in here, I promise. I just have to drop off these designs, and then we'll be on our way."

"I'm going to miss you tonight, but I can't wait to see Grandma and Grandpa again."

I was so thankful she had such a strong relationship with my parents.

"Grandma told me she's making your favorite for dinner."

She jumped up and down. "Spaghetti! Yay!"

As a single working mother, I always felt guilty when I had to leave her with my parents or a sitter during the evening, but I cherished our little dates when we went for ice cream and pedicures. She called them Lucy Days. And I especially needed one right now.

James's request had changed my plans a little. She'd called while I was picking Lucy up from school; she said she was flying home tonight and wanted to review the revised sketches as soon as she landed. Since they were boards, I couldn't email them; therefore, they had to be dropped off. James told me no one would be at her condo until this evening, so the doorman would let me into their elevator, and I was to leave the designs in the kitchen.

I never took Lucy on appointments, but because no one was home, I figured this one would be safe.

The elevator door slowly opened, and I walked into James's condo. "Stay right next to me, baby," I said, "and try not to touch anything."

Every few steps, I glanced in her direction, watching her eyes widen as she took in the view.

Lucy had been in nice homes before. Shawn's was absolutely stunning. His just didn't overlook downtown Miami from one of the highest buildings in the city, nor did it have a long stretch of ocean where boats were passing by. And, even though the little place we lived in was so close to here, our view was of another building with a strip of retail stores below.

"Wow," she said as she moved over to the windows.

"Baby, don't put your fingers on the glass."

I turned the corner, making my way toward the kitchen, holding the designs in my hands. I was so proud of the changes I'd made, and I had a feeling they were going to love them. Once the additions were approved, I would start working on fabrics and finishes, getting down to the details of each room.

"Mommy, look at the boat."

I took a quick glance behind me, trying to see what she was pointing at, but as I did, I heard, "Samantha," spoken in Brett's tone.

My attention was immediately pulled away from my daughter, and I looked to my right where Brett was walking down the hallway.

His eyes connected with mine, and my feet stopped moving.

"Brett, hi, *ummm*...James asked me to drop off the updated designs. She said no one would be home, so I didn't know you were here." I was so caught off guard, I was rambling.

"It's no problem," he said. "I just got home a little while ago." He nodded toward Lucy. "Who's this?"

I waited for her to join my side before I said, "This is my daughter, Lucy."

He stuck his hand out, his eyes fixed on her. "Nice to meet you."

"This is Mr. Young," I told her. "He's one of my clients. Can you say hi to him?"

She took his hand and even gave him a little bow. "Hi, I'm Lucy. Fancy to meet you."

God, I love that kid.

I was positive my brother had taught her that when he was feeling like being a smart-ass. But Lucy was unique, creative, extremely independent, and the fanciness really fit her.

"Here are the designs," I said, handing him the boards.

He took them from me, but his eyes never left Lucy, his lids even squinting like he was really checking out her features.

And then I watched an expression wash over his face. It moved from his mouth to his stare.

He had put it together. I knew for sure when his gaze shifted over to me, and he said, "I thought she was a toddler. We both did."

My heart was beating so hard, I swore, he could hear it.

I wrapped my arm around Lucy's shoulders. "No, she's seven."

I called her my little girl, my baby. *Is that why Brett thinks that, which means Jack thinks that, too?*

"I'm seven and a half, Mommy," Lucy said.

In any other situation, her response would have been cute. Brett probably would have laughed, and I'd have, too. But I was sure hearing her age only confirmed what he had already suspected.

"Her eyes," he said.

In that moment, I knew exactly what he was referring to.

They looked identical to Jack's.

There was no reason to deny it at this point. After this evening, the secret would be out.

I took a breath. "Lucy, why don't you go back over to the window and see how many boats you can count?"

After she skipped to the glass, I whispered to Brett, "I'm telling him tonight."

He raked his hand through his hair. "Jesus Christ, Samantha." He glanced at Lucy again and then back to me. "You're definitely going to do it tonight?"

"Yes."

"Because you're putting me in a hell of a situation right now." He tugged on the ends of his hair before his hand dropped to his side. "I won't lie to him, so if he doesn't know by tomorrow morning, I will tell him."

"He has to hear it from me," I said softly, reinforcing that he needed to wait and not say anything before I spoke to Jack. "Please, Brett, trust me when I say, I'm going to tell him."

He nodded.

I called Lucy over and said, "Are you ready to go get ice cream, baby?"

"Yes, I am."

"Please tell James she can call me anytime to discuss the new additions." I then looked down at my daughter. "Can you say good-bye to Mr. Young?"

She put her hand in the air, and she gave him a high five. "See ya later, alligator."

"After a while crocodile," Brett said, winking at her.

Then, we made our way toward the elevator and got inside.

When it closed, Lucy slipped out from under my arm, and she faced me. "I counted nine boats, Mommy."

"That's so great, baby," I told her, trying to hide the emotions from showing on my face, but inside, my body was revolting.

That never should have happened.

I shouldn't have brought her here.

And I shouldn't have put anyone in a situation where they had to make a connection between my daughter and her father.

The last thing I wanted was to hurt Jack, and Brett finding out first jeopardized that.

"What color toes are you getting, Mom?"

I couldn't continue looking at her while I was feeling this vulnerable, so I pulled my phone out of my bag and clicked on the screen. "Hold on a second, baby. I have to send a quick message."

Me: James's fiancé just met Lucy. He recognized her eyes and put two and two together. If I don't tell Jack by the morning, he's going to do it.

Anna: The positive news is that you're going to tell Jack, so he won't have to.

Me: I can't breathe.

Anna: Yes, you can. And you can do this.

Me: You have too much faith in me.

Anna: I just know what you're capable of, and you're one of the strongest people I know. You're going to handle this, too. You just have to get through tonight, and you will.

Me: Okay.

Anna: Call me after you drop off Lucy. And don't forget to breathe.

21

JACK

I NEVER ASKED Samantha what she felt like eating for dinner, but I knew I wasn't in the mood for anything fancy. All I wanted was to throw some substance down my throat, strip her clothes off, climb on top of the island, and have her sit on my fucking face. So, instead of messing around with appetizers and utensils and sides, I just ordered some pizza.

The doorman brought the cheese and pepperoni pies up a few minutes before Samantha arrived. When I was alerted that she was in the lobby, I grabbed two beers out of the fridge and brought them into the foyer where she was just stepping out of the elevator. Holding the bottles in one hand, I used the other to pull her toward me, crashing my lips onto hers.

I breathed her in, realizing how much I'd missed her smell since this morning, how much I'd craved her body, how just the feel of her made everything about today so goddamn perfect.

But, after a few seconds, something felt off.

She wasn't warm.

Her hands weren't on me.

Her body was stiff as hell.

I pulled back and handed her the beer. "You all right?"

She shook her head.

"Take a drink," I told her.

She looked at the bottle and gave it back to me. "I can't, Jack."

I did a quick scan, trying to see if I could tell what was wrong. She wasn't put together like she normally was. Her hair was on top of her head in a messy knot, she had on a pair of yoga pants, and she wasn't wearing makeup. She wasn't crying now, but her puffy eyes told me she had been.

She was still hot as fuck, but something didn't feel right.

Neither did her puffy eyes.

She wasn't crying now, but I could tell she had been.

My hand went to her waist, my thumb rubbing over the side of her navel. "Tell me what's going on, baby. Is Lucy okay?"

She stood frozen, her stare not moving from mine, her lips sealed shut.

I didn't know where this coldness was coming from.

After our talk last night, I'd forgiven her. I understood that she wanted to keep her daughter separate from the men she dated. I hadn't made a big issue of it, so it couldn't be that.

What could have happened between then and now?

"I can't do this when you're touching me." She gripped my fingers and pulled them off her.

"Do what?"

"Talk to you."

What the fuck?

Since she didn't want me near her, I turned and walked into the kitchen, setting her beer on the counter and holding mine near my mouth. "Talk."

She followed me, staying on the other side of the island where she'd eaten last night, where I'd kissed her, where I'd lifted her off the stool and carried her to my bed. But, now, I watched the emotions ripple across her face. Both arms wrapped around her stomach, and her skin was becoming pale.

"Samantha, what the fuck is wrong?"

I couldn't just stand here. I had to do something. I had to make this better. I had to let her know that, whatever she was feeling, I could fix. But, to do that, I had to be close to her, so she could feel the truthfulness in my words.

I went to move around the island, and she put up her hand to stop me.

"Stay there," she said. "At least until I get this out." Her fingers dropped to the counter, and she gripped the edge, her chest moving so goddamn fast as she breathed. "I don't know how to do this." Her voice was so fucking soft. "I've been rehearsing this over and over again in the car and on the phone with Anna and while I walked over. And, now, I'm here and..."

Who the fuck is Anna? What the hell is she talking about?

She finally looked at me, and the pain in her eyes stabbed my chest. "I don't know how to say it. I don't know where to even begin."

"At the beginning. That's where you start, but first"—I pointed at the stool—"you need to sit down."

If she didn't take a seat, I feared she was going to fall.

She pulled the stool out and set her ass on top of it. It looked like the movement exhausted her. "I have something to tell you, Jack. And I don't want you to say a word until I'm done."

I stepped forward until the counter was hitting my waist and held on to my beer with both hands. I didn't know what to expect, but I didn't think it was going to be good. "I'm listening."

22

SAMANTHA

REGRET MADE it hurt to breathe.

It made everything shake.

It made everything tighten inside my body.

I was looking into the face of this beautiful man, whom I had loved for the last eight years, and I knew my deception and my confession were going to alter the course of the rest of his life.

So, I continued to hold the counter. I rocked back and forth over the stool. And I took as deep of a breath as I could, knowing it might be the last time in a while when my throat wasn't fully restricted.

"I was just a kid," I started with. "Nineteen years old. Fearless. Unaware of consequences. Just having the time of my life. I knew how to get good grades, how to make friends, how to drink all night and still make it to an eight o'clock class. That was who I was when I met you."

Jack had placed my beer on the counter, and I grabbed it, guzzling the cold liquid, trying to keep my throat wet so that the tightness wouldn't completely dry it out.

"I had no intentions of falling for you during those three days

161

we hung out. We lived on opposite sides of the country. You were several years older than me, out of school, in a professional career. We were in two different places in our lives." I rolled the bottle around, watching the condensation leave a mark on the stone. "But, after we spent that time together, I really fell for you. I thought the feelings were mutual. So, when I left New York, I honestly thought we had a chance. At least, I wanted to try to make things work. That's why I texted you about me coming to LA. I had no idea that it would scare you off and cause you to shut down. I just knew I wanted to see more of you, and that was the only way to make it happen."

The words were getting harder to speak as the weeks following our trip to Manhattan became much fresher in my mind. All of that silence I had endured, all of those questions that had eaten at me, all of the unknown.

"It had taken you a while to text me back, and then I didn't hear from you again until you cut things off." I stopped moving the beer and looked at him. "I didn't expect to lose you completely."

"We've talked about this."

The sound of his voice startled me. "I know. I'm not punishing you, Jack. I'm just telling you again that I tried and tried to contact you. I sent emails. I left voice mails. And there was a reason for that." I swallowed and almost choked. "Three weeks after I saw you in New York, my period was late."

His eyes widened, and I knew he was making the connection. "I wore a condom."

"When I was late, the same thought ran through my head. There was no way I could be pregnant. We used protection. But, after days went by and I still hadn't started my period, I bought some tests, and they came up positive. All ten of them. I still didn't believe it, so I went to the doctor. Sure enough, he confirmed what I feared." I dropped my hands into my lap and

ENDORSED

squeezed them together. "Thirty-seven weeks later, Lucy was born."

"What are you saying to me?"

I'd thought about this moment since the day I heard her first cry.

At the time, I had been scared, young, and alone. I never felt like there was another option. But, as I looked into Jack's eyes, the same eyes that looked at me every day from the face of my daughter, I knew I hadn't made the right choice. I should have been stronger, more determined, more truthful, but I hadn't been. Now, I would pay for it for the rest of my life.

A knot was lodged so far into my throat, I could almost feel it with the back of my tongue. My eyes were starting to fill. My mouth was dry, and I couldn't swallow.

"What I'm saying is"—I tried to breathe—"Lucy is your daughter."

23

JACK

"THERE'S NO FUCKING WAY."

My head was spinning. I couldn't even think straight.

I'm Lucy's father?

The little girl of hers that she finally told me about last night?

The one I assumed was a hell of a lot younger than seven years old?

"She's yours, Jack."

"Impossible."

I didn't know what the fuck to do, so I walked to the fridge, grabbed two more beers, and set them on the counter. Screwing off the caps, I tossed the metal in the sink and wrapped my lips around the top of one of the bottles.

I didn't give a fuck that she was crying. I needed clarity. I needed someone to start explaining this to me before I lost my shit. "How in the hell did I get you pregnant?"

"You don't remember what happened before you put the condom on?"

The night began to unravel in my head. When we had been at the bar, I remembered taking the condom out of my wallet and

MARNI MANN

putting it in my pocket. I couldn't recall when I'd grabbed it from there, but I knew I'd put it on because I remembered throwing it away.

"No," I told her. "I don't know what you're talking about."

"You didn't immediately put the condom on. You weren't in me long without it, but it must have been enough."

"I did what—"

And then it came back to me. The tightness I'd felt. The warmth. The way her wetness had spread over my skin. It had felt so fucking good, but I knew I had to wrap it up, so I gave her three pumps—four tops. Then, I'd rolled the rubber on.

I pulled out the stool and sat my ass on top of it, both hands running through my hair as I thought about what this meant. "I want a paternity test."

"No problem," she whispered. "I'll do whatever you want."

I still couldn't believe this.

That I had a child.

That I'd had one with Samantha.

That she was just telling me about her now.

"You're positive she's mine?" I asked.

She nodded. "I'd only been with one guy that year, and it happened months before you."

How the hell am I supposed to process this?

Especially while she sat in front of me with tears running down her face like she had a reason to be sad. Like she wasn't the fucking cause of this.

"Why didn't you tell me?" I asked through gritted teeth.

"I tried."

"You tried?" Anger was exploding in my voice, and I didn't stop it. I didn't give a shit about her feelings or if I was upsetting her more. Because this wasn't about her; this was about me. "You didn't try hard enough."

She sucked in a breath, her teeth gnawing on her bottom lip.

"I left you six voice mails. Six, Jack. I sent you emails. And all of that came after you told me you didn't want to talk to me again."

"I can't believe you just fed me that line of bullshit." I gripped the bottle, and my teeth ground together.

"I didn't know what else to do. I couldn't reach you. You wouldn't respond. You didn't want my brother to know anything had happened between us. Should I have told him his brand-new agent was my baby daddy? Would you have called Shawn back?"

"Fuck you. You're unbelievable, you know that?" I squeezed the bottle so goddamn hard, I was waiting for it to break. "You had my child inside you. I don't give a shit if I was his agent or not." I got off the stool and backed up until my ass hit the sink. "You should have told me. All you said was you needed to talk to me in those messages, but you know damn well what you could have said that would have gotten me to return your calls—something like, *I'm fucking pregnant, Jack. Call my ass back*, would have worked just fine."

"Jack, you're right; I don't want you to think I'm blaming you. I should have told you. I should have found a way. There's no question about it; I fucked up. But I was a kid. I didn't know what I was doing. I just knew I was pregnant by a guy who didn't care about me, who wanted nothing to do with me, and I had to be strong for the baby. I did the best I could."

My heart was thumping through my chest, my pulse was racing, and a scary mix of emotions was shackling my goddamn brain. Every justification she had given me made it all worse.

"Samantha, you kept my fucking child from me."

"Jack—"

"We would have figured out a way to talk to your brother and your family, and we would have made it right. But you took that option away from me. And you took seven years of her life away from me."

"I know." She wiped her face with her sleeves. "I'm so sorry."

167

"If I hadn't seen you at the Super Bowl, would you have ever told me?"

It appeared like she was thinking about my question, but she was shaking her head. "I don't know."

My arm went back, my fingers twisted around the bottle, and I tossed it as hard as I could toward the wall. It flew through the air, beer spilling onto the floor, and when it smashed, it made the loudest noise.

The only sound that followed was Samantha's sobs.

I looked at her and hissed, "Get the fuck out of my house."

"Jack, I—"

"Get the fuck out, Samantha. I don't want to see your face."

Her tears were streaming faster. Her lips and her chin were quivering.

I didn't give a shit.

Every drip that came from her eyes only disgusted me more.

The sight of her did, too.

"I know it was wrong. I know I should have tried harder. I'm so sorry—"

"Sorry isn't good enough."

She stood and backed up to the far side of the kitchen. "How can I make this right?"

I shoved my hand in my pocket before I searched for something else to throw. "You can't. You've done enough damage. Now, get the fuck out."

I heard her rush through the living room and go into the foyer, her fingers pounding on the button for the elevator.

Before it opened, I had a question to ask, so I moved into the next room, which gave me a full view of her. "Samantha?"

She glanced over her shoulder with the tiniest bit of hope on her face.

There was no reason for that.

I wasn't going to throw her a goddamn bone.

"Yes?"

"Are you going to let me see her, or do I have to hire an attorney?"

She put her hand over her mouth for a few seconds, and then she gradually moved it down. "Just give me a chance to tell her first. Once she knows, I promise I won't keep her from you."

Now, she wouldn't.

How fucking nice of her.

"Get out!" I roared again and turned around, heading straight for the bar that was on the other side of the living room.

I lifted a bottle of scotch, twisted off the cap, and held it to my lips. The liquor burned my throat, but it was the only thing that was going to make me feel better tonight.

24

JACK

"JESUS FUCKING CHRIST," Max said. He finished off the scotch I'd poured for him and then added, "I can't even wrap my head around this shit."

I felt the same way, which was why I'd called the guys and Scarlett shortly after Samantha left and asked them to come over. Since they'd arrived, we'd been sitting in the living room where they ate the pizza I'd ordered, and I filled them in on everything that had gone down.

Getting it all out seemed to help, and having them here made me calm again.

Exploding like I had earlier would only make this situation worse.

"How did I not know any of this was going on?" Max asked.

He looked at Brett and Scarlett, and she responded with, "I just found out, too. You weren't the only one."

"There wasn't anything to tell," I replied. "Samantha and I reconnected at the Super Bowl. Once I had a better idea of where things were going, I would have told you."

"I know you're looking for advice," Max said. "But, man, this is a tricky one. I think it's important you get a paternity test. At least then, you'll know for sure."

"I asked her for one, but I already know what it's going to say. Samantha wouldn't have told me unless she was positive."

"What's your opinion, Scarlett?" Max asked.

She took her heels off and put her bare feet on the ottoman, running her fingers through the ends of her hair. "As a woman, it's your responsibility to tell the father of your child regardless of your relationship with him." She glanced at me. "But I can't pretend to know what she went through or what that would have felt like or how scary that would have been at nineteen." She sighed. "That's what I keep going back to—that she was only nineteen. You're a baby at that age, and you don't know a decision that massive will affect the rest of your life."

Silence passed between the four of us.

We'd been through so much together—deaths in our families, career-ending decisions, financial turmoil. A kid was one we hadn't dealt with yet. I had known it would come one day, especially with Brett and James getting hitched. I just hadn't thought I'd be the first to have one.

A child.

Fuck, it still hasn't set in.

"I can't believe she never reached out to tell you," Max said.

That was the part of the story I'd left out.

"But she did," I told them. "She texted several times. She left me voice mails. She even sent a few emails."

"And you never got back to her?" Max asked.

I shrugged. "No."

"That's fucked up of you," Scarlett said.

I nodded. "I know."

Brett walked to the bar, refilled his glass, and came back. He didn't sit. He stood in front of the large sectional and stared at me. "Samantha came to my condo today to drop off some sketches. She had Lucy with her."

My feet dropped off the cushion in front of me and fell to the floor, my body sitting up straight. "You met her?"

I didn't even know what she looked like.

What she sounded like.

I hated that he had seen her before me.

"The second I saw her, I knew. Of course, it helped that I was expecting a toddler, and she was far from that," Brett said, looking like he was going to turn a little soft on me. "Jack, she's beautiful. She's got these huge blue eyes that are identical to yours and the same shape of your face. She's got her mother's lips but your smile."

I exhaled. Loudly.

And I tried not to let his description hit me too much.

"Did you say anything to Samantha about this?"

"Hell yeah, I did. Once I called her out, she admitted it and said she was going to tell you tonight. I followed that up with an ultimatum and said if she didn't tell you by tomorrow morning, I would."

Any person in this room would have done the same.

"What time did this happen?"

He seemed to think about my question and finally answered, "Around three this afternoon."

Samantha had texted me about dinner long before that, which told me running into Brett had sent her over the edge. That was the change I'd felt in her when she showed up at my place.

"She's a cool kid, Jack," Brett continued. "Smart and sassy, like James would say. She even shook my hand. I was only with her for a few minutes, but I can tell Samantha raised her right."

I couldn't believe he was talking about my kid.

That she had my eyes.

That she lived in Miami.

"Fuck, this is complicated," I said.

Brett sat on the end of the couch, his elbows resting on his knees. "I'm going to agree with Scarlett on this one. Samantha was young; she didn't know what the hell she was doing. It sounds like she even lied to her family about who the father was. When you blew her off, she could have gone to her brother to track you down, outing you in the process. Instead, she chose to keep what you two had done a secret, and she had a baby entirely on her own. That took some balls, Jack."

"Yeah, it did," Max said.

I pushed myself forward on the couch and gripped the sides of the cushion with both hands. "She didn't have to do it on her own. I would have been there for her, had she told me."

"Jack, we know that about you, but not everyone responds the way you do," Scarlett said. "Samantha obviously didn't feel the same way. I think you might need to cut her a little slack because, to me, it sounds like she tried to tell you."

This was coming from a woman and my best friend and someone who always had my back.

As pissed as I was at Samantha, I needed to hear this.

And I needed to consider how she felt.

"You were pretty rough on her, brother," Brett said. "I could tell she was panicky at my place, so I know it couldn't have been easy for her to come here and confess."

"Look, she fucked up; we all know that," Max said. "But you fucked up, too. You can't just point your finger at her."

I had been rough on her.

I'd thrown a goddamn bottle at the wall.

I'd kicked her out of my house.

I'd told her I would get a lawyer if she didn't let me see Lucy.

"You know, if we're being technical, this whole thing is your fault," Brett said.

Max and Scarlett looked at me, waiting for me to react.

But I didn't. I let Brett finish his thought.

"What fucking idiot sticks his cock inside a chick when he doesn't know if she's on birth control?" He took a drink. "You know better than that. We all do."

I did know better, even at that age.

Fuck, especially at that age.

I just hadn't thought those few pumps would do anything.

Man, was I wrong.

"You need to think about everything that happened tonight," Scarlett said, hugging her arms around her stomach. "Break it all down—the things you said to her, what you want, how you see this moving forward. Then, you need to address it with her. Just don't make any irrational decisions when you've been drinking."

"In other words, don't fucking call her tonight," Max said. "And don't throw any more glass."

"I won't." I shook my head. "But I was so fucking angry, and I'm still so fucking angry. I lost seven years of her life."

Max pulled his tie, loosening the knot from his neck. "I get it, but she's not just some random chick or a baby mama you want nothing to do with. You wanted to be with her before you found out she'd carried your child. Now that you know, that's got to change things a little."

I didn't know what it did.

My mind wasn't ready to go there yet.

Scarlett's hand landed on my arm, and she said, "Do me a favor; don't come into the office tomorrow. With Brett and Max flying out, that gives me a whole day without the three of you, so I'll actually be able to get some work done."

Brett laughed. "She's tired of us harassing her about the celebrity alert."

"That's true," Scarlett admitted. "Although I would have said this anyway." She made sure she had my full attention. "You found out some life-altering news today. You need to get your head straight. So, go do whatever you need to do, but don't come in."

"In all the years we've worked together, I don't think you've ever given anyone the day off," Max said. He looked at me. "Take that shit and fucking run, man."

"I'm a hard-ass. This is why you love me." She poked the same arm she'd been holding. "I mean it. Take some time; you need it."

"All right." I checked the time on my phone, and it was close to midnight.

The guys were flying out before eight tomorrow morning, and they were going to be on the road for close to a week. They needed some sleep.

"Get your asses out of here. I've kept you long enough," I said. I stood, leaving my scotch on the end table, knowing I'd had more than enough, and I walked Scarlett and the guys to the elevator. "Thanks for coming. You know that shit means a lot to me." I slapped hands with Max and Brett, man-hugging each of them, and then I kissed Scarlett on the cheek. "I'll be in touch with you guys tomorrow," I told them.

When they were all in the elevator, Brett pointed at me. "Think about what we said. It'll be worth it in the end."

25

SAMANTHA

I STOOD AT THE STOVETOP, mixing the noodles around the boiling pot, staring at my daughter, who was sitting on the counter next to me. This was how we'd been making dinner since she was four years old. Lucy would hang out in the kitchen, telling me about her day—some parts fictional, some not. And I would listen, proud of the little lady she was turning into, encouraging her to use her big-girl words, to be a leader among her friends, to be creative and independent, like I had become.

It was always just the two of us.

A team.

Anna was a huge part of Lucy's life. My parents were, too, and my sisters and Shawn, but for the most part, it was just her and me.

That was going to change.

She would now be spending time with her father, a man I'd spoken about like he no longer existed, and that had satisfied the mind of a seven-year-old.

I was nervous for her.

I was even more nervous for me.

177

"So, at Grandma's house," Lucy said, "we watched this show on lions. Do you know…"

I zoned out, trying to pay attention to what she was saying, but I couldn't.

My mind was on Jack.

The anger on his face, the hatred in his voice, the way he had looked at me like I was only out to hurt him. Enough that he had threatened to get an attorney.

I wasn't going to keep Lucy from him. Once she knew the truth, Jack and I could work out visitation, so he could see her.

And, even though he wanted nothing to do with me, I hoped, for the sake of our daughter, he would try to get along with me.

My plan was to start the conversation with her after dinner tonight. Since she'd spent the last two evenings at her grandparents' house and her homework was already done, we were going to eat and talk about this man, Jack, who had come into my life. Then, we'd watch her favorite movie and have cookie sandwiches with buttercream frosting for dessert.

We'd discuss him a little more tomorrow and the next day, building it up, getting her comfortable with the idea, so it wouldn't come as quite a shock when I eventually told her. Once I felt like she was ready, the two of them would meet.

But I couldn't rush this, not with her.

She was too young, too innocent, too gentle.

He would have to understand that. Knowing Jack, I was sure he would.

God, he had missed so much.

Major decisions. Big moments. So many accomplishments.

All because of me.

I stopped stirring for just a second to look at her beautiful face. As she continued to speak about her time at my parents' house, I tried to imagine what her reaction would be when she met him. Whether she would immediately warm up to him or if it would take a while for them to connect.

He was so charming and charismatic; I had a feeling they would be best buds after their first time hanging out, and she'd fall right in love with him.

Like I had.

The thought stabbed my chest with something sharper than anything I had in my kitchen.

I'd lost him once, but during that time, I hadn't seen him.

Now, he was going to be in my life; he just wouldn't be with me.

Knowing that was going to make this so much harder.

But the only person I could be angry with was myself.

And I was.

"Mom?" Lucy said, dragging my attention away from the pasta, which I hadn't realized I'd been staring at.

"Yes, honey?"

"I'm glad I'm not at Grandma and Grandpa's house tonight and that I'm home with you."

"Oh, yeah?"

She nodded her small head. "I missed you. A whole lot."

She always knew the right thing to say.

"I missed you, too, baby." I put the spoon down and held out my arms. "I could use a really big hug right now."

She pushed off the counter and fell against my chest.

I caught her.

I always would.

No matter who came into her life.

Or mine.

26

JACK

I STEERED the boat toward the marina, pulling up next to the dock, just as one of the assistants came over to tie me to the boat lift.

"Are you done for the evening, Mr. Hunt, or do you plan on going back out?"

I stepped onto the dock after I cut the engine. "I'm done for the night." Reaching into my pocket, I grabbed the twenty that was in there and slipped it into his hand. I headed for my car, driving out of the parking lot to go home.

I'd been on the water since noon. That was over nine hours ago, and I wasn't sure where I'd gone, which inlets I'd driven by, what islands I'd stopped at. I just knew I'd done a hell of a lot of thinking, and somehow, I'd gotten myself back to the marina where I kept my boat.

Scarlett had given me the best advice last night by telling me not to come into the office. So, I'd spent all of today trying to clear my head.

Twenty-six hours had passed since I found out about Lucy.

And things were finally starting to sink in.

I was still angry, but I knew it wasn't going to buy me time with my daughter. It wasn't going to give me back what I'd lost.

Now, I just had to move forward.

But, first, there was something I had to do.

Apparently, my brain wanted it done immediately because, when I shifted into neutral and went to turn my car off, I wasn't in my parking garage. I was outside Samantha's building instead.

I glanced through the glass and up at the thirty-plus stories.

Lucy had school tomorrow; therefore, I assumed she was already in bed. That meant, Samantha was either working from home or watching TV or soaking in a bath. But she was up there, somewhere, behind one of those windows. And I hoped to hell she was willing to talk to me.

If I called or texted, I was worried she wouldn't respond. The only way to do this was to see if she would let me inside.

I got out of the car, locked it behind me, and headed down the sidewalk.

There was a doorman standing out front, and as I approached, he said, "Can I help you?"

I shoved my hands into the pockets of my shorts. "I'm here to see Samantha Cole."

"Miss Cole hasn't notified me that she's expecting any visitors tonight. I'll have to call her and get your visit approved. Can I have your identification please?"

I pulled out my wallet and handed him my license.

"Wait here," he said, and then he went into the lobby. Standing at the desk, he held my ID while he spoke into a phone. He glanced in my direction, said a few more words, and hung up. When he came back outside, he returned my license and said, "Mr. Hunt, Miss Cole has asked that you give her a call."

I found her number in my cell, and I hit the button to call her.

As I took a few steps away from the door, she answered and

said, "Jack, I'm not trying to keep you away from Lucy, but she's sleeping right now, and I don't want our conversation to wake her."

"Samantha, listen to me, I didn't come here to argue with you. I'm past that. I know you wouldn't keep Lucy from me. I just want to talk to you."

"Besides my father and brother, no man has ever been inside my apartment. If she came out of her room and saw you or heard you—"

"She's my daughter," I said in the calmest voice I had. "I'm not going to do anything to upset either of you. She won't hear me, nor will I wake her up. You have my word."

"Okay. Then, put Larry back on the phone, and I'll tell him to let you in."

"Thank you." I turned around and handed him my cell. "It's Samantha."

"Miss Cole," he said and paused. "Very well. I'll send him right up." He gave me back my phone and signaled me to follow him into the lobby. "Miss Cole lives in unit six-two-nine. Head left when you get to her floor. She's about halfway down the hall."

I nodded and went into the elevator, pressing the button for the sixth floor. I got off, and once I reached her door, my hand lifted to knock, but I stopped before my knuckles hit. Not wanting to wake Lucy, I sent Samantha a text to let her know I was outside.

Only a few seconds passed before the door opened.

"Hi." Her voice was so small, and she appeared just as tiny as she stood in the large doorway. She had on a pair of shorts, no makeup, and a pair of glasses that had thick black frames.

"Hi, Samantha."

"You can come in, but please remember to be quiet. She isn't a soft sleeper, but if she hears you—"

"I told you, you don't have to worry."

She stared at me as though she were assessing my demeanor, and then she opened the door wider and moved out of the way, so I could enter. I stayed close behind her, keeping my eyes on the ground, not wanting to see anything related to Lucy.

I just wasn't ready for that yet.

She took us through what I thought was the living room, into a short hallway, and to the door at the end. Once I stepped inside, she flipped on the lights to reveal a bedroom that I assumed belonged to her.

"Lucy's room is on the opposite side of the apartment, so this gives her the least chance of hearing us."

She was taking every precaution.

She moved around me and sat on the bed by the pillows. "You can take a seat or stand. Whatever you want."

She appeared even tinier on the huge king-size as she hugged her knees to her chest, her bare feet resting on the gray comforter.

I stayed in the center of the room and glanced at the windows and her furniture and the bathroom behind me, making sure to avoid all the pictures in case they were of Lucy. I wasn't sure what to do with my hands, so I shoved them in my pockets, like I'd done downstairs. "I'm angry, Samantha. Maybe not as angry as I was last night, but I'm still furious that I lost seven years of her life. That being said, we have to move forward. I'm not sure I can ever forgive you for keeping her away from me, but for Lucy's sake, I'm going to try. As for last night, I shouldn't have thrown my beer, and I shouldn't have kicked you out. It wasn't right."

"I delivered some of the most shocking news a person could get. I'm not surprised you had a strong reaction."

"I'm usually not a man who lets his emotions get the better of him."

I watched her movements on the bed, the way she squeezed

herself tightly, how it looked like she was preparing for something.

I was sure she was confused as hell.

That was my fault.

Now, I needed to try to fix it.

"I've thought a lot about everything you told me," I said. "I've gone over it so many times in my mind. What I should have done differently, what I should have said, and what you should have said." I shook my head. "Fuck, if we could only rewind this to eight years ago."

"Jack, if only I could change the—"

I cut her off with, "We don't have to go back there. I just want to move on, and I'm coming to you because I don't know the best way to do it."

Her arms dropped to her sides, and her hands pressed into the bed. "Slowly. That's what I think is best."

I nodded, knowing that was probably a good approach. "When are you going to tell her?"

"I already started to."

"You did?" I was surprised she'd moved so fast, considering how long it had taken her to tell me. I walked closer to her and took a seat on the edge of the bed. "What did you say?"

She spread her legs out and crossed them. "It was after dinner, and we were cleaning up. She was telling me about one of her friends, so I told her about one of mine. I just said that there's a guy in my life named Jack. And that he's sorta neat."

She knows my name.

I took a breath, letting that settle in.

I took another as I thought about her sleeping on the other side of this apartment. There was no attachment yet. I didn't even know what she looked like. But there was something in my chest that tightened whenever my mind went to her.

"She asked if you were my boyfriend." Her cheeks turned red.

"What did you tell her?"

"I didn't give her an answer."

Silence passed between us, but I could feel her questions in the air, and I had so many of my own.

"I want to know her," I said as I thought about Lucy's eyes that Brett had described to me. "I want to know what I missed out on. I want to know what you looked like when you were pregnant. I want to know who was with you in the delivery room. I want to know her full name. I want to know what time she was born. I want to know what her first word was. I want to know her favorite color. I want to know her favorite food. I want to know if she plays any sports."

She started to sob, and it gutted me.

"Don't cry, Samantha. I don't want you to be upset. I want us to get through this."

"I just messed this up so much, Jack."

As I looked at her, the mother of my child, I realized that I would always be angry with her, that nothing she could say would make what she had done right. But, in that moment, I also realized I had fallen for her.

I was so confused by these emotions—the anger and the love mixing together. It was messing with my head.

Can we make this work?

Can I walk away from her and only be Lucy's dad?

Or can I go back to where we had been just a few days ago and know that, on top of loving this beautiful woman, I will have a daughter to love, too?

"You did, Samantha, but this is our chance to start over." I gazed at her legs, my stare eventually moving up her stomach and to her face. "I came here tonight, prepared to discuss where we'd go next with Lucy, but as I sit here, listening to you, watching you, I know my feelings for you haven't changed."

"You still want to be with me?"

"I don't want to be without you."

She exhaled loudly. "You make it sound so easy."

"It is because I've wanted you from the moment I saw you at the Super Bowl. That was before I knew you had a daughter, and even that didn't change my feelings. And, now that I know she's mine, we can only get better." I reached forward and put my hand on her foot. "This can be easy, Samantha. I want her, I want you, I want us."

Her mouth opened. Nothing came out of it.

But so much emotion passed through her eyes. I needed to know how she felt.

When I couldn't take it any longer, I broke the silence, "Samantha, say something."

"I don't know what to say." A tear dripped onto her trembling lip.

"Baby..."

More tears fell down her cheeks. It took everything I had not to reach forward and wipe them off.

"You're telling me you want to be with me, which means I get to give my daughter a father, something I'm positive she's always wanted, and I get to have you for myself, too."

I nodded and backed it up with, "Yes." I glanced to my left, seeing a frame on a small end table. I couldn't bring myself to look at what was in the middle of it. "I know there are pictures all around your room. If Lucy is in any, I don't want to see them. The first time I look at my daughter's face, I want it to be in person."

She continued to gaze at me, the emotion just piling up. "How about you come over on Saturday? That will give me a few more days to talk to her about it and get her ready."

"I'd really love that."

"Okay." She stood, using the backs of her hands to wipe her face, and she took several steps toward the end of the bed. "I need a second."

"Samantha—"

"Just a second. This has all been a little too much."

As she tried to pass me, I clamped my hand around her wrist, causing her to stop and look over her shoulder.

"Don't go."

"Jack—"

"Come to me instead."

27

SAMANTHA

"COME TO ME INSTEAD."

I heard his words in my head, and I felt how serious he was in the way he gripped my wrist.

But going to him meant not running off to the bathroom where I would cry into my hands, where I'd eventually put my face under the faucet and try to calm myself down so that I could return to my room. That was what my emotions were pushing me toward—tears and quietness and air that didn't have Jack in it.

Because, even though I'd listened to his confession, I still couldn't believe it.

He wanted my daughter.

He wanted me.

He wanted us.

I was getting everything I'd dreamed about, and I couldn't hold it together. There were tears, spit, and even snot.

I was a mess.

But he looked at me like I was the most beautiful woman he had ever seen.

He squeezed me harder and said, "Samantha, come to me."

189

I felt myself moving.

I saw the distance between us close.

I heard his breathing as his body was suddenly pressed against mine.

"It's your turn to tell me what you want."

Since I'd left his condo, I'd only thought the worst. My mind had returned to the pain I'd felt eight years ago, and I'd begun to go through it again until all of that changed a few minutes ago.

"You," I whispered through tears, several of them falling over my mouth. "Just you and Lucy. That's all I've ever wanted."

He lifted my chin, so I was now looking at him. "I want to kiss you." He exhaled, and I smelled the spiciness of his cologne. "But, because Lucy is in this apartment, I'm asking for your permission."

He'd kept every promise he'd made when he called me from downstairs.

My lids shut, and I felt more wetness on my face. I took a breath and opened my eyes again. "Kiss me, Jack. Please. Make all the pain go away."

His lips didn't smash against mine, nor did he grip me with the kind of power that he normally used. Instead, he was gentle, completely in tune with what I needed, giving me the softness I craved from him tonight.

His tongue teased mine, his hands rising until he finally cupped my cheeks, swiping the tears with his thumbs. Then, he used his palms to wipe the rest of it, eventually pulling away to press his nose into mine.

He breathed.

My eyes stayed closed as I was filled with his scent again.

"Her first word was *cat*," I told him, my bottom lip starting to quiver even harder.

"Cat," he repeated, as though he were trying to hear her

voice. He kissed down my neck and stopped underneath my chin. "Because you had one?"

"No." His mouth felt so amazingly good, it was hard to hold in the moans, yet there were still tears, plenty of them, streaming down the sides of my face. "Her favorite book had a cat in it, and I read it to her every day."

"Samantha..." He continued to kiss my neck until he reached the other side where he went up to my cheek and stilled. "Let them fall, baby. I'll lick every one."

It was too much—his tenderness, his touch.

His love.

His tongue flattened, and he swiped up several. Then, his hands held my head back, and I felt his lips press against my collarbone and gradually work up until he reached my mouth. "I want to make love to you."

Since Lucy was born, I'd felt him inside my apartment. Every time I gazed into my daughter's eyes, it was like staring directly into his.

And, now, he was here.

In my bedroom.

He wanted me, and I wanted him.

I'd heard everything he'd said to me, but I needed to feel those words. I needed his touch to make me whole again.

"Jack," I said, tasting a tear as it fell onto my tongue, "I need you."

He dropped to my chest, caressing and licking the spots not hidden under my tank top.

When I finally looked down, my eyes connected with his. Goose bumps spread across my body as he breathed into my skin.

"Her favorite color is blue."

He breathed again. Deeper this time. "Titans blue?"

"Yes, that exact one for that exact reason."

His hands went to my ass, and he lifted me into the air,

wrapped me around his waist, and carried me to the bed. He placed me in the middle of it.

With my lips still on his, I said, "Her favorite food to eat is Italian."

"Just like her mom."

As he kissed me, he took off my tank and pulled down my shorts. I wasn't wearing a bra or panties. The only thing that covered any part of me was my glasses that shielded my eyes.

If I took those off, I wouldn't be able to see him.

He tossed his polo shirt onto the floor, finally showing me the body I'd been thinking about since I last ran my hands over it. He had broad, muscular shoulders and a well-defined chest that sprouted a thin layer of dark hair. A set of abs followed, each one indented and outlined, and toward the bottom of his torso, a V cut across his sides and disappeared under his waist.

He was perfection.

Once his shorts were off, he pulled a condom out of his wallet and climbed back over me. When he kissed me, it was so soft. A subtle touch of his lips. The gentle brushing of his skin on mine.

I felt him place the foil in my hand, and then his mouth went to my chest, moving across each breast. He spent much more time with my nipples, grazing those with his teeth, sucking them against his tongue.

"She was born at three ten in the morning," I said as he went across my navel. "And Anna, my best friend, was in the delivery room with me."

He kissed the very bottom of my stomach. He kissed the center. He kissed over the right side and left, covering the entire section where Lucy had lived.

My tears leaked onto the comforter, and I said, "Jack, I was huge when I was pregnant with her."

"But I bet you were beautiful. I wish I could have seen you."

He moved in between my legs, spreading them apart,

resting them over his shoulders. Then, his lips pressed against the top of each thigh, going as far as my knees and back up, never getting near my folds. He was taking his time. Tasting, loving. And I was taking in every kiss that he pressed against my body, letting them fuel my emotions, the tears falling even more freely.

Slowly, he moved closer, and I was ready for it. He licked around my lips, pointing his tongue as he rose through the center, eventually flicking the spot at the very top that I liked him to touch the most.

The pleasure spread across my throat and to my breasts and throughout my whole stomach.

My body was melting from him.

And, with every swipe of his tongue, I released a little bit more of the heaviness that had been weighing me down for so long.

With every press of his lips, I felt us moving past the anger.

Because of that, I could start forgiving myself.

Suddenly, my body was more sensitive than it had ever been.

So, when he slipped his face away and his beard scraped my inner thighs, I groaned so loudly.

"Someone's not being quiet," he said.

I gripped the blanket between my fingers, wiping the wetness from my cheeks. "I've just missed you so much, Jack."

"Baby..." he said so softly again.

He continued to feast until I tugged his locks so hard, he was forced to work his way back up, his beard tracing the path on my skin. When he reached my chest, his hand went to my face, and it rubbed in the droplets that had fallen in the last few seconds.

He was healing me with his body, the same way I wanted to heal him with my words.

I had to give him more.

I had to give him the moments he'd missed.

I nuzzled my face into his hand and said, "Her favorite sport is swimming."

"Swimming?" he said as though he were surprised. "I can't do anything with swimming." He smiled, and it was so beautiful. "Maybe I can get her a full scholarship, but the potential of going pro is—"

"She's seven."

"We need to start her young."

I laughed through more tears.

His mouth went to mine, and he turned us, so he was sitting by the pillows with his back against the headboard, and I was kneeling in front of him.

He nodded toward the condom, so I ripped the corner of the packet and pulled it out. I positioned it over his tip and rolled it down until the latex reached his base. Then, I climbed on top of him, slowly working him into me.

He was holding my face steady, his thumb on my lips, so he could feel every exhale that came out of my mouth.

The words I was about to say would vibrate over the pad of his finger.

They would hit him the hardest out of everything I'd told him so far.

I closed my eyes, I slowed my movements, and then I connected our stare. "Her full name is Lucy Jacklyn Cole."

He looked at me with so much adoration in his eyes. "Jacklyn?" he whispered. At first, it sounded like a question, but then his expression told me it had sunk in, hitting him the way I thought it would.

He wrapped me up in his arms, holding me so tightly, and the both of us started trembling.

"Jack, I—"

"I am, too."

My mouth crashed into his, and I breathed him in as I moaned.

He made the same noise, holding my cheeks like he couldn't let go, and I knew we were coming together.

When we finally stilled, when it was only our panting that filled the silence, we were still clinging to each other. Our hands and our mouths were so desperate to be close.

"One last question," he said, each syllable tickling my face as his nose leaned into mine.

I pulled back a few inches to get a better look at him before I placed my hand on his beard. He gave quick, tender pecks to the sides of my fingers, and then his eyes closed just briefly. When they opened again, they were full of tears.

"Do you think she'll love me?"

A sweet sigh escaped my lips, water pouring from my own lids.

My heart was so full of love for this man.

I ran my hand under his eyes, catching each drip before they fell. Then, I leaned my face into the side of his, hugging him with everything I had, and I whispered, "How could she not?"

28

JACK

Me: *I listened to all of your advice, and I went over to Samantha's place tonight.*
Brett: *Did you meet Lucy?*
Scarlett: *That's exactly what I was just going to ask.*
Me: *She was sleeping. It's better that she was. I wasn't ready to tackle both girls in the same night. First, I needed to smooth things out with Samantha. The plan is to meet Lucy on Saturday.*
Max: *How smooth did you make things with her?*
Me: *I want to be with her, and I told her.*
Brett: *And?*
Me: *And she didn't kick me out. Well, shit, she eventually did because she didn't want Lucy to wake up in the morning and see me in her mom's bed. We didn't think that would be the best introduction.*
Scarlett: *I'm proud of you. I'm proud of her. Now, I think I speak for all of us when I say, we want to meet Samantha and this gorgeous niece of ours whose eyes I'm going to eat up.*
Me: *Samantha first. Lucy will come soon, but she needs to get used*

to me before she meets all of you. Let's get together—James, Eve, and Vince, too.

Max: Eve is coming to Miami next week. Pretty sure she's flying with James.

Scarlett: I'll talk to Vince, but I'm certain we can make something work for next week.

Brett: I'm so fucking happy for you, brother. Long time coming. This girl's the right one.

Scarlett: I second that.

Max: Third.

Me: Much appreciated. I'll see you guys when you get back. And, Scarlett, I'll be in the office tomorrow. I don't need any more time off.

29

JACK

"JACK HUNT," I said to the doorman as I reached the front entrance. "I should be on the list to see Samantha Cole."

He checked his tablet, and then he opened the door for me. "Do you know her unit number?"

"Yeah, I'm good," I replied over my shoulder as I walked in and went over to the elevator, pressing the button for the sixth floor.

I'd been thinking about this elevator ride for the last few days. How it would feel when I reached her hallway, when I knocked on her door, and when she let me in.

That was because I wasn't just meeting my daughter today. Samantha and I were also going to tell her that I was her father.

Since I'd left here a few nights ago, Samantha and I had been talking several times a day, and we'd weighed every option. She went back and forth on what would be best. She asked friends. She consulted with Lucy's pediatrician. What she decided was to assess how the day was going. If things were all right, we'd tell her.

I couldn't describe what was happening inside my body.

I just knew I was standing inside the elevator, staring at the numbers above the door, waiting for the goddamn thing to slide open. I knew my hands didn't feel comfortable hanging at my sides or in my pockets or resting on my biceps as I crossed my arms.

As I shifted between my feet, the number six lit up.

The elevator stopped.

The door opened.

My eyes dropped down, catching the piece of art that hung on the wall across from me.

I inhaled, and I let the air sit in my lungs for a few seconds before I blew it out.

This wasn't a meeting about endorsements. This wasn't a negotiation. I wasn't going to be sitting across the desk from a CEO or a professional athlete or a marketing team.

This decision-maker was probably going to be the most observant and intuitive one I'd ever met.

And she was only seven years old.

I left my confidence in the elevator, and then I made my way down the hall, halting when I reached her apartment. I knocked gently, and my hand moved to my side again. It felt misplaced, so I hooked it into my back pocket.

A few seconds passed before I heard the click of a lock and the twisting of the handle. As the door swung open, I expected my gaze to fall on Samantha's gorgeous face.

But her eyes weren't the ones looking back at me.

The ones I stared into were identical to mine.

Blue.

Sharp.

And so fucking bright.

"Lucy," I heard myself whisper.

She was a tiny little girl, wearing a pink dress, with long, dark hair like her mother's and full lips and a small nose.

Her smile was like mine.

The dimple on her left cheek—Jesus, she had gotten that from me, too.

"You must be the Mr. Jack Mom says is coming to hang out with us today."

Her voice.

It was a little high-pitched and soft at the same time and so goddamn sweet.

"I am."

"Then, it's fancy to meet you, Mr. Jack."

She stuck her hand toward me, and I saw the blue polish on her nails and what appeared to be flour on a few of her knuckles.

I delicately gripped her fingers. "It's pretty fancy to meet you, too, Lucy."

Lucy.

My daughter.

"Mom's taking cookies out of the oven. She says I'm too young to do that, so we're on decorating duty." She waved her hand in the air, as if she were welcoming me inside their apartment. "Would you like to decorate cookies with me and my mom?"

I didn't tell her that I never had.

Because it didn't even matter.

Right now, I would do anything that little girl asked.

"I would love to," I answered.

Her bare feet patted on the floor as she skipped into the kitchen. "Mom, Mr. Jack's here. He wants to decorate cookies with us."

Samantha was standing in front of the open oven, reaching inside to pull out a cookie sheet. She gazed at me as I stood in the entryway and mouthed, *Sorry.*

I was sure she was apologizing for not answering the door. As it turned out, I wouldn't have had it any other way.

"Hey," I said and leaned into the wall, glancing from her to Lucy.

She set the cookie sheet on the counter and took the mitts off her hands. "Hi." With her eyes locked on mine, she said, "Lucy, did you introduce yourself to Mr. Jack?"

"Yes, Mommy. We're already friends."

I laughed, surprised by Lucy's response.

"Is that so?" Samantha inquired.

"Yeppers." Lucy came over to where I stood and put her fingers on my arm, tugging me deeper into the kitchen. "First, we wash your hands." She took me to the sink and turned on the water, picking up the bottle of soap and squirting some onto my palm. "Lots of soap. That's what Mom says."

I rubbed my hands together, and then I held them under the faucet, feeling Lucy's eyes on me, positive that Samantha was watching me from behind.

"Done," I said, showing her my clean but very wet hands.

She handed me a dishcloth. "Yay, let's decorate," she squealed.

I smiled as I dried my fingers and followed her to the island. I'd been so focused on my daughter that I hadn't paid attention to what was in all the bowls on the counter. There was frosting in several colors and different kinds of sprinkles and candies.

"This is my favorite part." She lifted a cookie off the rack and placed it in front of her.

I watched as she spread the icing over the top with the precision of a surgeon. Her little tongue poked out as she carefully scattered the sprinkles.

She had marvel in her eyes, scanning the cookie all over, and when her masterpiece was complete, she declared, "It's done." She took another, placing this one in front of her, too. "I'm going to do a blue one now." She looked at me. "Mom says we can send some to Uncle Shawn 'cause he loves my cookies, and blue is also his favorite color."

"Lucy," Samantha said, placing more on the rack, ones that she'd just taken out of the oven, "do you know that Mr. Jack works with Uncle Shawn? He's his agent, which means he helps Uncle Shawn get deals with companies that want to work with him."

She glanced up from the frosting, her mouth open in awe. "Like the camera one?"

"Yes," I told her. "Just like the camera one."

"That's *sooo* cool."

Samantha's cell started ringing from the other side of the kitchen. She hurried over to it, lifted it into her hand, and stared at the screen. "Jack, I have to take this."

I spread some blue icing over my cookie, making sure it was all even, getting most of it on my fingers. "It's fine; go ahead."

"You're sure?"

I could see how terrible she felt about leaving us.

I nodded. "Don't worry."

With the phone in her hand, she rushed out of the kitchen and headed in the direction of her bedroom.

When I heard the door close, I said, "How do you think I did?" I held the cookie up for Lucy to inspect.

"More blue there," she said, pointing to the left side with a finger that was completely covered in frosting. "Then, it'll be so perfect."

I picked up the spoon again, spreading more over the spot she'd pointed at, running the metal back and forth until I was sure it was all even. When there wasn't any cookie showing through, I reached for the blue sprinkles and dusted just the outer edge.

"Yours is going to be really pretty." She poured half a handful of sprinkles in the center of hers and moved to the next one. "Looks like it's going to taste really good, too."

"I hope so," I told her. "I'm hungry, and I love cookies."

"Mom will let us have one when we're done, but only if we promise to eat *all* of our dinner..." She paused and looked toward the living room. When she glanced back at me, she said in a quiet voice, "She's making pasta. And I *looove* pasta."

Italian.

I knew that.

Her hand hovered over the frosting bowls. "Mr. Jack, what color do you like the most?"

"Red."

She grabbed that spoon and scooped up enough to cover three cookies. "I'm going to make this one for you."

I shook my head, smiling. "Thank you."

She leaned closer to me to grab some chocolate chips. "Hey, you wear that smelly stuff that Uncle Shawn wears."

I laughed as I remembered spraying on cologne when I'd gotten out of the shower. "I do."

"Grandpa doesn't wear anything that smells. He says it gives him a headache. Uncle Shawn wears lots of stuff, but his doesn't smell like yours."

"No?"

I knew the kind Shawn wore.

That was another endorsement I'd secured for him.

"Pinkie promise you won't tell Uncle Shawn this secret?" She held out her hand, her littlest finger extended.

I wrapped mine around it, and she did a little shake. "I promise."

"He smells like that one time Mom took me up north to see snow, and those trees with the long leaves—the ones that look like needles, ya know? He smells like those kinds of trees, and it makes me sneeze."

A trip I had missed.

The next time she went north to see snow, I wanted to be with her.

I wanted to take her skiing.

Fuck, there were so many things I wanted to do.

"My mom always tells me my dad smelled real good."

Goddamn, they'd been talking about me.

I closed my eyes for just a second, quickly opening them because I didn't want Lucy to see, and I busied my hands with another cookie. "What else has your mom told you about him?"

She reached for the red sprinkles and dumped several piles over the chocolate chips. "That he was the most handsomest man in all the land. That he smelled good, he traveled all over the place, and that I have his eyes." She turned toward me. "I love when I go to bed, and she tells me stories about my dad. He's a really, really important man."

I heard footsteps in the kitchen that didn't belong to either of us, and I slowly glanced over to the doorway, meeting Samantha's smiling face.

She laughed. "What are you two whispering about?"

Lucy faced her mom. "I told Mr. Jack he smells good and that you always say my dad smelled real good, too."

Samantha's chest began to rise and fall really fucking fast, her stare shifting over to me with so much emotion in it.

I knew nothing about timing.

Even less about children.

This had to be her call.

And, whatever she decided, I would support.

With even more emotion in her voice, Samantha said, "Let's go to the park for a little while. We can take some cookies with us to eat there."

Lucy jumped up and down. "Yippee! Mr. Jack, I *caaan't* wait to show you my favorite slide."

We spent a few hours in the park, playing on the slides and the swings and the balance beams. All three turned out to be Lucy's favorites. When Lucy started getting hungry, we went back to their apartment, and we helped Samantha cook dinner. We were just finishing up eating when Samantha gave me a slight nod.

It was time.

Today had gone better than I'd imagined, and I could tell Samantha agreed.

But, man, I didn't know how she was going to break the news. Or how Lucy was going to take it. Or how the fuck I was going to react when she voiced it to Lucy.

"Lucy," she started, "we want to talk to you about something very important."

Lucy glanced up from her plate with sauce all over her face. "Okay."

Samantha hadn't touched much of her dinner. I hadn't really eaten mine either, but she had moved her plate to the spot next to her, so she could rest her hands on the table.

"Do you remember what I told you about your father?"

My gaze shifted between both girls.

One had blue eyes that were so fucking wide, and the other was trying to hold back her tears.

"Yes, Mommy. You told me you liked him a whole lot, but after you and Daddy met, you never saw each other again. And, if he knew I was born, he would love me very much."

I couldn't calm my breathing. My heart felt like it was exploding inside my chest.

If I had known she was born.

Fuck.

This hurt so much worse than I'd thought it would.

But this moment was between Lucy and her mom. Samantha

needed to get this out. She had to be the one who told our daughter. So, for now, I was just going to listen and observe.

"That's exactly right." Samantha took a breath. "At Uncle Shawn's Super Bowl party, I saw your daddy again."

Her eyes lit up. "You saw him?"

Samantha nodded. "Yes, baby."

"Did you talk to him?" she asked, sounding so interested.

"Yes, and I told him all about you, and he was so sad he didn't know you were born, but he's been dying to meet you and be a part of your life."

"He is? Is he coming to see me?"

I couldn't stay silent anymore. I had to be the one who told her this. She needed to hear it from me.

I swallowed and cleared my throat, not knowing what I would sound like when I finally said the words. "Sweetheart..." I waited for her to look at me. "I am your daddy."

Her eyes widened even more. "You're my daddy?"

I didn't know how a seven-year-old would process this.

I didn't know if there would be tears or questions.

Or anger.

But Lucy just continued to gaze at me, waiting for my answer.

"Yes, I'm your dad. And I'm so sorry I haven't been here. Please understand that, if I had known about you, I wouldn't have missed a day of your life."

I was trying so fucking hard to keep the emotion out of my eyes.

I wasn't the kind of guy who felt things this strongly.

Who teared up over shit like this.

But this little girl had changed something in me.

She made me feel different.

And the way she was looking at me right now told me she was feeling some of that, too.

I wasn't just a guy who worked with her uncle Shawn, who liked the color red.

I had a title.

And it was one she hadn't called anyone before.

She put her fingers on my arm, and I felt the stickiness of the pasta. "Can we see you whenever we want?"

We.

"Yes." I tried to say more, but when I opened my mouth, my breathing cut me off, and I coughed.

Samantha must have been able to tell because she said, "Your dad is going to be here forever, baby. He's not going anywhere."

I silently thanked her, and she nodded.

"Do you have any questions?" Samantha added. "Because your daddy and I know this has to be very confusing for you. We want to know how you're feeling, and we want you to talk to us about it."

With her eyes on me, she put one of her fingers into her mouth, like she was thinking really hard. "What do I call you now?"

"You can call me whatever you're most comfortable with."

She didn't respond right away but finally said, "How about Jack?"

"I like that," I told her.

I didn't expect her to immediately call me daddy, but I hoped, one day, she'd love me enough to consider it.

"I like it, too," Samantha said.

"Mommy, can Jack move in with us?"

I quickly glanced at Samantha and watched her reply with, "Right now, we're just going to focus on you spending as much time with Jack as possible. How does that sound?" She smiled.

So did our daughter.

"Jack, can you pick me up from school one day? And come to my swim lessons? And come watch me at ballet?"

"Yes," I said, "to all three."

My heart didn't feel any more settled. If anything, that shit was racing like I'd just finished running ten goddamn miles. But I knew, while I glanced between these two gorgeous girls, that this was going to work out somehow. That this was the start of our father-daughter relationship.

And, even though I'd only just met her, I had a love for this little girl that I'd never felt before.

Lucy stood from her chair and came over to mine. Without warning, she threw her arms around my neck and tucked her small head into my chest. "I've always wanted a daddy. I'm so glad you found me."

30

SAMANTHA

Jack: Are you ready for tonight?
Me: As ready as I'll ever be.
Jack: Max and Scarlett are dying to meet you.
Me: Will I need to worry about Vince talking smack? I mean, my brother did destroy him in the Super Bowl.
Jack: Did I just hear your competitive side?
Me: Do you like it?
Jack: I just pictured you in your glasses and those little fucking shorts you had on and the way I could see your nipples through your tank top.
Me: Wait until you see what I have planned for tonight.
Jack: How long do I get to keep you out for?
Me: All night.
Jack: The teenager from downstairs isn't watching Lucy?
Me: No, Anna is, and she's staying until the morning.
Jack: Fuck.
Me: All those hours to do whatever you want to me...
Jack: Stop teasing me.
Me: Why? Because I said, whatever you want?

Jack: Samantha, I'm warning you.
Me: I'm not scared.
Jack: You should be.
Me: I'll see you at 7.

AS I LOOKED in the mirror, Lucy and Anna watching me from the bed, I twirled to the right and then to the left to see myself from every angle.

The two of them had helped me get ready, curling my hair, weighing in on the colors of makeup I should use. Lucy had even picked out my shoes and clutch. I wanted her to be involved as much as possible. The last thing Jack and I needed right now was for her to feel left out.

Since she'd learned Jack was her father, she'd seen him almost every other day. He'd come over for dinner or taken the both of us out. Last weekend, we'd returned to the park and gone to the beach. We'd even taken a late-night swim in the rooftop pool upstairs.

During all that time, Jack and I hadn't really been alone much. I was being too cautious, I knew that, but having him in my apartment after Lucy went to sleep made me extremely nervous. I feared she'd wake up to look for me and find us in my bed—naked.

I couldn't let that happen.

The time our daughter spent with Jack had to be about her, not me.

But, after rescheduling several times, his friends were finally all in town along with their significant others, and Jack wanted me to meet them.

This would be our first date since he'd found out about Lucy.

I couldn't help but wonder if things would feel different now that all of our time had been spent with her. His texts were always flirtatious. Our phone calls, when we weren't discussing our daughter, were a little steamy. But that could change the second we were alone. He could look at me now as just Lucy's mother and not the desirable woman he once had.

"Samantha, you look smoking," Anna said from the bed. I glanced at her in the mirror, watching as she said to Lucy, "How do you think Mommy looks?"

"*Sooo* pretty," Lucy replied, cuddling into Anna's side.

In the last few weeks, since Jack had come into her life, I'd noticed a huge change in her. She smiled whenever I mentioned him; she got so excited whenever she knew she was going to see him.

She was as smitten as I was.

And I knew her love for him would only grow.

As would mine, and that thought made me a little nervous, too.

There were so many things I still needed to tackle, like telling my family the truth about Jack. But I was getting there even if I was just taking baby steps.

The sound of the doorbell chimed, and Lucy jumped up from the bed. "Is that Jack?"

"Sure is, baby," I said.

"Can I go get the door, Mommy?"

"Of course."

I heard her feet pounding on the hardwood floor as she raced to the door.

"Hi, Jack!" she squealed loud enough that Anna and I could hear.

Anna stood from the bed and came over to me. "She loves him."

"He loves her. Wait until you see them together now. He's so enamored; he won't say no to anything she asks, and he just beams when he looks at her."

"Oh God. I didn't think that man could get any hotter. Apparently, I was wrong."

Anna had been working so much lately, her shifts sometimes going late into the morning, so she'd only had a chance to meet Jack once.

She grabbed my clutch off the dresser and handed it to me. "You need to hurry up in here, or I'm going to go out there and steal your man."

I took the purse from her and did another turn.

"You're looking at yourself like you're doubting what you have on. It can't be the dress. You seriously look stunning. So, what's going on?"

"I'm just a little nervous; that's all."

"Nervous? Why?"

I played with the ends of my hair, twisting them into one large curl and resting it over my shoulder. "This is our first solo date since he found out about Lucy. Plus, I'm meeting all of his friends tonight, and two of them are my clients."

"Call me slow, but I don't see why any of that would stress you out. With the way you look, I'd be surprised if Jack doesn't try to get you naked in the car on the way there. And, Samantha, everyone adores you; you've never had a problem with getting along with people, so why would tonight be any different?"

I kept my voice low and said, "They all know I lied about Lucy."

"Oh."

"Exactly my point."

She put her hands on my shoulders and turned me toward her. "Listen to me, Jack has gotten past it, and he's the one who really matters. I don't think he would put you in a situation where people were going to be tough on you or judge you." She held me tighter to reinforce her words. "You're going to go out, have some much-needed cocktails, and dance your little ass off. So, stop worrying, or I'm going to spank you."

I put one of my hands on top of hers. "I love you."

"I know."

"Brunch tomorrow? Just us? I've missed you."

"Where's Lucy going to be?"

I lifted her hand off me but linked my fingers through hers and walked her to my bedroom door. "You'll see."

We stood in the doorway, watching Jack and Lucy on the couch. She was sitting on one of his legs, leaning back into his chest while she showed him something on my tablet. He had his arm around her, his chin resting on top of her head, and he was laughing at whatever she was pointing at.

"I think I just came," Anna whispered. I gently hit her arm and glanced at her. "What? Don't even tell me you didn't because I know you'd be lying."

I didn't come, but my heart certainly melted. The way he looked at her, the way her attention never left him, the similarities in their features—it was beautiful.

And seeing Jack as a father was the biggest turn-on.

"Girl," Anna whispered close to my ear, "you'd better have some of the freakiest fucking stories to tell me about over brunch. I need details of you and that man together. I'm talking sweat, sounds, places his tongue touched your body—I want all of it. So, do me a favor, and make me proud tonight."

I laughed a little too loud, causing Lucy and Jack to gaze in my direction.

"You have my promise," I whispered back, and then I stepped into the living room, watching Jack take me in.

"Wow," he said, his eyes glued to my body. "Lucy, your mommy looks gorgeous."

"She does," Lucy said from his lap. She tilted her head, so she could glance up at him. "I wish you were taking me, too, Jack."

My heart.

This time, it melted for an entirely different reason.

Jack gently lifted her, turning her whole body to the side so that her neck wasn't strained, and he smiled at her. "I have an idea," he said. "How about, tomorrow morning, you and I go for pancakes?"

"Pancakes? I love pancakes. They're my favorite. But Mommy never lets me get the chocolate chip ones."

He smiled harder. "You know what that means, don't you?" he asked her. "I think, tomorrow morning, both of us need to order the chocolate chip pancakes, and we can take pictures and send them to your mommy."

"I just came again," Anna whispered from behind me.

"Yay!" Lucy shouted, her eyes immediately shifting over to me. "Mommy, I can go, right?"

She was still processing that Jack was her father. At some point, I was sure she'd stop asking me permission to do things with him. And, eventually, for day-to-day decisions, she'd ask the both of us. It would just take time.

"Of course you can, baby," I told her. "Jack and I will be back in the morning, and that's when he'll take you. Anna will be here to help you get dressed."

"Yippee!" Her arms went around Jack's neck, and she gave him the biggest hug.

He kissed her on the cheek and said, "Have fun with Anna tonight."

"Thanks, Jack," she said, releasing him.

I held out my arms, and she pushed off his lap and rushed to me, holding me so tightly. "Baby, be good for Anna tonight. Jack and I will see you in the morning."

"Okay, Mommy."

I kissed her cheek. "I love you."

"Love you, too."

As Lucy started to move away from me, Anna said, "We have pizza to order and cookie sandwiches to make. Who's ready?"

"I am!" Lucy sang.

I gave Jack a signal that told him it was time to go, and he stood from the couch and made his way over to me. As Anna brought Lucy into the kitchen, we waved good-bye to them and slipped out the door.

"That little girl has me wrapped right around her finger," he said, his hand on my lower back, the other one making sure the handle was locked.

"Yes, she does, but it's adorable."

We weren't more than a few steps down the hall when he grabbed me by the waist, turned me toward him, and pushed my back against the wall.

"I've been waiting too long to do this." His lips crashed against mine, and I was filled with his scent.

God, I'd missed it.

And his lips.

And his touch.

And the way my body responded every time his hands were on me.

I moaned as his fingers moved up my sides and around my back.

"You feel so good; I don't know if we're going to make it to the bar. I might just take you back to my place instead."

He still wanted me. Nothing had changed.

I closed my eyes and felt that bit of worry begin to leave my body.

Still, I knew we couldn't go straight to his place, so I gently poked his chest and said, "Getting all of your friends together has kind of been a nightmare. We cannot reschedule on them."

He ducked his face into my neck and kissed down to my collarbone. "They'll understand."

My head pushed back, and I sighed from the wetness that was already starting to pool between my legs. "Jack, we're going."

"Fine, but only for a little while," he murmured. "And then..." He squeezed my ass so hard. When he lightened his grip, I expected him to move to a different part of my body. But he didn't. He slapped the spot he had just clutched, and he growled, "This is mine tonight."

31

JACK

SINCE THE MOMENT we'd shown up at the club in South Beach, my friends hadn't left Samantha alone. Max was completely charmed by her, and I had a feeling that, whenever James and Eve and Scarlett were all in town, the four women would be having a girls' night.

It made me so fucking happy to see how well she fit in, especially because I knew how apprehensive she had been. What she soon learned about my friends was that they didn't give a shit about her past. They didn't judge her for her mistakes. They accepted her for who she was now, and they loved her.

Once Samantha, Eve, James, Scarlett, and Vince had gone to the dance floor, which was at least thirty minutes ago, Max and Brett hadn't been able to stop talking about her. They were asking even more questions about Lucy.

They wanted to meet her, and tonight, they were pushing hard for it.

I needed to talk to Samantha about doing a dinner at my condo where everyone came to us. But, right now, all I could think about was burying my cock inside her.

That fucking thought got interrupted when Brett said, "I'm going to need you guys to get fitted for your tuxes soon."

"I didn't know you'd picked a date," I said.

"We're getting closer to securing one. We're just trying to work it in between James's filming schedule."

"She's fully booked?" Max asked.

"You have no fucking idea. Everyone wants her."

"Every time James mentions Eve's name in an interview, she lands more celebrity clients. That girl is blowing up, too."

"That just means more time away from Miami," Brett said.

Max didn't respond, so I said, "Thank fuck I don't have that problem."

"Nah, but you've got two girls to make happy, and that comes with its own set of problems."

I laughed and glanced out toward the dance floor, seeing Samantha wedged between James and Scarlett. Vince was behind Scarlett, and Eve was just to the side of them.

I shot back the rest of my scotch and set the empty glass on the table. She'd met them, and she'd danced. Now, it was time I had her all to myself.

"I'm going to grab Samantha, and we're out of here."

Max held out his fist, and I pounded it. "We'll see you at the office on Monday."

I did the same to Brett's fist. "You got it, buddy."

I made my way out of the VIP area and went to the dance floor, carefully weaving around the crowd. With Samantha's back to me, she didn't see me approach, but she felt me the second I wrapped my arms around her waist and put my lips on her neck.

"Mmm," I growled. "You look so fucking hot right now."

Her hands went to my arm, holding me in place, and she turned her head to kiss me. I took her mouth in the roughest way, and her body ground against mine.

Knowing how my lips affected her made my dick even harder.

I pushed my cock into her, so she could feel what she was doing to me. Then, I leaned into her neck again and said, "It's time to go."

She gave me the sexiest look as I slipped back a few inches. "It definitely feels that way."

"Girls," Samantha said, getting their attention, "Jack is dragging me home, but I had such a blast with all of you."

"*Nooo*," James cried, giving Samantha a hug. "You can't leave us."

"Girl, we're having dinner in a few weeks once I get back to Miami," Eve said when it was her turn to embrace Samantha.

"Yes," Scarlett agreed, hugging her last, "dinner is a must."

Samantha kissed Vince on the cheek, and he said, "It was great to meet you. Even if you are Shawn Cole's sister."

We both laughed, and then I escorted her toward the back of the club where there was an exit that led to the parking lot.

"Did you have fun?" I asked as we got outside.

She smiled, chewing the corner of her lip. "I had the most incredible time."

"Good."

My gaze dropped down her body, at the strapless dress that hugged her gorgeous tits and her small waist and the best fucking ass.

I took her to the passenger side of my car and opened the door to help her inside. Once she was in, I slipped into the driver's seat and started the car, shifting into first.

When my hand wasn't on the gearshift, it was on her thigh. Her skin was hot. Tight. But it didn't give me the heat I was after, so I went to search for it, dragging my fingers higher on her leg. My thumb then dipped below the hem of her dress, tracing a small pattern over her flesh.

"Samantha, I need you to do something for me."

She took a breath that ended with the softest moan. "Okay."

"I need you to shift when I tell you to."

"Why?"

"Because I need one hand on the steering wheel while the other is inside your cunt."

"Jack..."

"Shift into third."

She quickly reached across my arm, grabbing the gearstick and moving it like I'd asked her to.

My fingers climbed several inches higher, feeling the space widen as she spread her legs apart. "Now, go to second." As I rose to the outside of her pussy, I expected to feel her panties.

There was nothing.

Just a bare pussy and a clit that needed me to rub it.

"Jesus," I hissed. "Neutral. Shift right now."

We were coming to a stop at the red light. Before the car completely slowed, my pointer finger traced around her entrance to wet the tip, and I slid right in.

"Oh my God," she groaned. "Your hands."

She'd missed them.

They'd missed her.

And she was about to get a hell of a lot more.

She slipped her other hand around my wrist, pushing me even deeper inside her. As I got further in, the back of her head leaned into the seat, exposing her entire neck, and her mouth opened.

The lights around the car lit up the skin on her chest and throat, and I could see every breath she took, every swallow she made. And, each time she gave me a moan, I drove in to my knuckle and back to the tip of my finger, the slickness of her pussy dripping down to my palm.

When I saw green, I said, "First. Go."

Her head came off the cushion, and she put it into gear.

As I released the clutch, I gave her another finger. "Second."

She shifted and groaned, "Jack..."

"Third," I said, adding another, twisting my hand as I pulled back and again when I stroked in.

"Oh, shit."

"Fourth."

"I'm going to come."

I pushed my palm against her clit, staying inside her, letting her ride this out.

And she did.

Her nails fucking stabbed my wrist as each shudder shot through her, her cunt clenching my goddamn fingers like she was trying to juice them.

When I felt her orgasm pass, I pulled my hand away and licked my fingers, so I wouldn't soak the gearshift.

"You are..." she started, but her voice trailed off.

Each time I stuck my tongue out and swallowed, I felt her stare at me even harder. I didn't look at her until we reached the next light. "I'm, what?"

"You are...everything? Let's go with that. I don't think I can form any other complete words yet."

I laughed and gently set the tip of my thumb on her leg, grazing the outside of her thigh, feeling the goose bumps rise in every spot I touched. "Tell me something, Samantha. Are you on birth control?"

She nodded. "After what happened with Lucy, I've been getting the shot every three months."

"Good, because I wasn't excited about wearing a condom tonight."

"I was going to tell you once you realized I wasn't wearing any panties, but that happened before we got to your condo."

"I couldn't wait. I needed your pussy."

"I love that about you."

I turned my head straight and shifted into first, going slow toward the parking garage so that my car wouldn't bottom out. When I drove into my spot by the elevator, I turned the engine off and went to her door, not even waiting for her to put her feet on the ground. I just reached inside and pulled her into my arms. I carried her through the entrance that led to my private elevator.

I waited for the door to open, and I pushed the PH button as soon as it did, lifting her dress so that she was able to straddle my waist. Then, I put her back against the wall and fucking devoured her lips.

She tore at my shirt, not bothering with the buttons, just tugging until each one popped off and hit the floor. Once it was fully open, she pulled it over my shoulders, and it fell from my arms. My belt and jeans followed, loosening both enough so that I was able to get them to my ankles, slipping out of my shoes at the same time.

Leaving the pile in the elevator, I moved her into my condo, finding the first surface to set her on. It turned out to be the dining room table. With her ass now resting against the glass top, I unzipped the back of her dress and slithered it down her body.

"Do you want me to keep these on?" She was talking about the spiked red heels on her feet.

"Fuck yes," I barked.

I lifted her off the table, and my boxer briefs immediately dropped to the floor, my cock springing up, it was so fucking hard. I walked out of them and brought her to the nearest wall. Her hands squeezed my shoulders, and I bounced her on my tip a few times before I thrust inside.

"Goddamn it, you're fucking tight," I hissed, working back and forth, trying to loosen her enough so that my whole shaft would fit in.

When it did, I was swallowed by her warmth, her wetness,

the walls of her pussy that felt like a fucking tongue licking me over and over.

"Oh God," she breathed so loudly, and I joined her.

I wanted her to come.

I wanted her cunt pulsing around my cock.

So, I used my fingers to gently squeeze her clit, giving it just the amount of pressure she needed to explode.

When I felt her start to build, my hips ground in a circle, twisting halfway in to give her a different kind of sensation. My thumb ran down the center of her clit, and I fucked her with so much goddamn speed, so much power. Within a few strokes, I felt her completely unravel.

She screamed, "Jack!"

Her pussy squeezed me, and I plunged in deep, giving her hard, fast pumps to push through her orgasm.

"*Ahhh*," she moaned, and I slammed my lips against her, tasting the pleasure on her tongue.

I slowed when I knew she was coming down, and once I felt her loosen again, I carried her to my bed and set her on top of it.

She relaxed her body over the comforter and leaned onto her elbows. "I hope you're not seriously thinking about putting a condom on now," she said as I walked to my nightstand.

I gave her a small smile and showed her the bottle of lube I'd lifted out of the drawer. "I told you I was taking your ass tonight."

I squeezed a generous amount onto my shaft, making sure it was thickly coated, and then I crawled on top of her. "Have you done this before?"

She shook her head, and I felt my balls ache.

I fucking loved the idea that I was going to be her first.

"I'll be gentle."

She took a breath. "Where do you want me?"

"Right where you are."

I lifted her legs, so they were on either side of me, and I ran my hand down her pussy, gathering the wetness to bring it to her ass. I worked around the rim, dipping the pad of my finger inside, getting in as far as my center knuckle and pulling out. With my other hand, I flicked her clit, and her hips rocked back and forth in response.

"That feels so good," she groaned.

If she thought I'd ever hurt her, she was so fucking wrong.

Anything I did to her body, even if it was inside her ass, would give her the most intense pleasure.

I'd always make sure of that.

With an entire finger inside her, I added a second and moved my wrist in a circle to stretch her a little. When it felt like she could take more, I slid out, and I slowly pressed the tip of my cock against her. Easing my hips forward, I went in an inch and paused.

"Ah," she gasped.

I put my hand on her cheek. "I know this doesn't feel good yet, and I know it's probably uncomfortable, but trust me, it's going to get better in a few minutes."

I stayed in that spot, not moving, running my finger over her clit to give her more of the sensation I knew she enjoyed. And then, so fucking gently, I went in a little more.

"Breathe," I told her.

She was strong as hell, but she didn't have to be with me.

Each inhale she took, I slid in just a tiny bit, continuing that pattern until I was fully buried.

"Try to relax your muscles," I told her. "I know that feels impossible, but once you get used to me, it's going to feel better than you think."

I kept my finger on her clit, trying to get her to focus on something other than the fullness in her ass. With my other hand, I dragged my fingertips up her navel, squeezing her nipple, and I gave her just the slightest movement of my cock to start working in some of the friction.

"Ah," she groaned a second time, but it wasn't filled with the uneasiness I'd heard earlier. Now, there was pleasure in her voice.

"That's it, baby. Just a little bit longer, and it's going to feel fucking amazing."

She put her hand over mine, forcing me to pinch her nipple even tighter. "Wow, Jack, I never thought it would feel this good."

That was when I knew the discomfort was gone, and her eyes told me she could handle a lot more.

So, I shifted back and glided in, giving her short, easy strokes. "Fuck," I roared.

I couldn't help the noises I was making. She was so snug, and my cock was so wet from the lube.

I moaned even louder when she started to pulse around me.

"Jack..."

"You like it, don't you?"

Her hands were now on my thighs. She wasn't squeezing them or digging her nails into my skin. She was pulling me like she wanted me deeper.

"Yes," she hissed. "You're going to make me come again."

I knew it wouldn't take much.

Her hips were already bucking each time I swiped her clit.

And I knew, if I put a finger in her pussy, she would clamp around it like a fucking vise.

So, I did. Then, I reared my hips back, and I drove into her ass with as much speed and power as I had. I didn't stop when I heard her scream. I didn't slow when I felt the tightening inside my balls. I held her legs wide, and I worked out my orgasm.

"Jack!" she shouted.

I released her thighs, and I fell forward, catching myself with my hands before she got any of my weight. "Kiss me," I demanded.

She leaned up, and her lips crashed against mine. I pumped out each squirt of cum until I emptied myself in her ass.

I kissed her as I pulled out.

I kissed her on the way to the shower.

And I kissed her while I walked us under the water.

"That was incredible," she sighed as she tilted her head back into the stream.

I pressed my lips against her throat, and I exhaled, "I'm not done."

32

SAMANTHA

I'D REACHED the final step, and I knew this was going to be the hardest one to take.

That was because it was time to tell my brother that Jack was Lucy's father.

I'd already informed my parents and sisters. Jack and I had done it together. I wanted him there, so he could hear me tell them it wasn't his fault. That I was the guilty one. That I was the reason this had been a secret for so long. I deserved to take all the blame, and I wanted to make sure they didn't pass any of it onto Jack.

But they didn't.

They took it exactly the way I had expected them to. There was shock, disappointment. There was even surprise when I told them Jack and I had reconnected. They were pleased to hear our relationship was growing and that Lucy would now have her father in her life.

It would take them time to work through it all.

I understood that.

Before we left my parents' house, I made everyone promise

not to tell Shawn. I had to be the one to do it. And I was going to do it in person.

My parents had offered to watch Lucy while Jack and I went to Nashville, so I'd dropped her off at school this morning, and my parents would pick her up later today and keep her overnight. Jack and I would return to Miami tomorrow.

This was the first time we were leaving Florida together, the first time I was flying in The Agency's plane.

But this certainly wasn't how I'd envisioned our first vacation.

Still, doing this in person felt like the only way. I just didn't know how Shawn was going to react to the news, or if it would affect the way he felt about Jack.

The unknown was terrifying.

Jack's assistant had coordinated this entire trip, so when we got off the jet, there was an SUV waiting for us on the tarmac. We climbed into the back seat while our two small bags were loaded into the truck, and then the driver began making his way out of the airport.

"Shawn isn't expecting us for another hour," Jack said, brushing a piece of hair out of my face. "We have time to go to the hotel and check in if you want."

I looked out the window at the city I hadn't visited in what felt like forever, a place I should have been at for every one of Shawn's home games.

I'd avoided Nashville.

I'd avoided every stadium my brother had played at.

All because I'd feared I would run into the man whose arm was snaked around my body.

God, so much had changed.

I faced him and said, "Let's go right to Shawn's. I just need to get this over with."

He searched my eyes for several seconds before he instructed the driver. When he finished telling him our destination, he pulled me against his side and rested his chin on top of my head. "Stop worrying."

I sighed. "That's impossible."

My relationship with Shawn had always been different than the one I had with my sisters. We weren't just siblings; we were friends. We told each other almost everything. We talked about the people in our lives, and we gave each other advice.

I never felt the need to keep anything from him.

Until this.

And this was bigger than anything that had ever happened to me, and it had been going on for eight years.

I just didn't want to hurt him.

The thought of that absolutely killed me.

Because, during the time when my belly had been growing bigger every day, when my food cravings had been more important than going to class, when I had been worried about how I would graduate, Shawn was the one who had called me every night to get me through it. He'd coached me. He'd made me focus on the positive, and that was the little girl I would be bringing into this world.

We rode the rest of the way in silence, and I took in every building we passed, every sign, every curve in the road. I knew we were nearing his place when the houses began to get larger, and the lots were spread further apart, gates now blocking the entrances from the road.

The driver pulled up to Shawn's, and he rolled down his window. He spoke our names into the call box, and when the gate opened, he wound down the long path.

My brother was opening his front door just as my feet hit the ground, and I was met with his smiling face.

I walked over and gave him a hug, squeezing him longer than I needed to. "God, I've missed you."

"It's so good to see you," he said. "Now, are you going to tell me why you guys are really here? And why you're staying in a hotel and not with me?"

He knew something was up.

I wasn't surprised.

I pulled away, so I could look at him. "I think I need a drink first."

"Sam, it's ten in the morning."

"I know."

"Are you all right?"

I didn't have time to answer because Jack joined us, and he said, "Shawn, how's it going, buddy?" He clasped hands with my brother and gently slapped him on the shoulder.

"Real good, Jack." He took a few steps back. "My sister wants a drink. Do you want to booze it up, too?"

Jack gazed at me. "I'll just have some coffee. But I'll get it. I know where you keep it."

Shawn waved us inside. "Come on."

Jack put his arm around me and pulled me close. "You haven't eaten anything. Just be careful because it's going to hit you hard."

"It's okay. I need it."

We entered the house and went to the kitchen where Shawn began opening a bottle of champagne. Jack left my side to go make some coffee, and I watched Shawn work the wire off the top and pop the cork.

He filled a glass halfway and handed it to me. "Cheers."

I took the champagne over to the kitchen table and sat down, slowly sipping it so that I wouldn't get light-headed.

Shawn was looking inside the fridge and said, "Do you want anything to eat—"

"Shawn," I cut him off. "Come here."

My eyes followed him as he moved across the kitchen with his own coffee mug and sat in the seat next to mine. I waited for

Jack to finish making his coffee and join us before I said, "I really need to talk to you, and I can't wait a second longer to do it."

It wasn't the intro I'd planned, but it had certainly gotten his attention.

He glanced at Jack and then back to me. "Okay."

"I—"

"I'm Lucy's father," Jack spit out prior to me saying the words.

He knew how hard this was for me, and he was doing everything he could to make it easier.

The news passed over Shawn's face. I didn't see anger, but I could tell he wasn't pleased. "You're not telling me anything I didn't already know."

My eyes widened. "Wait. You already knew? Did Mom and Dad tell you?"

"Mom and Dad knew?"

"No." I looked at my glass. I wasn't sure if I had it in me to take another drink. "I just told them a few days ago. No one knew, except for Anna...and you apparently." I shook my head, confused by all of this. "How did you know?" My voice was so soft, I barely recognized it.

He leaned into the table, exhaling loudly. "I always had a feeling Lucy's father wasn't a one-night stand. You're not the one-night-stand kind of girl, Sam." He folded his fingers over the side of his mug. "I didn't put it together until Jack came to visit me here after the Super Bowl."

"How in the hell did you do that?" Jack asked. "I didn't even know Lucy was mine at that point, so it couldn't have been from something I said."

"It wasn't," Shawn replied. "Well, that's not entirely true. When I mentioned Lucy's name, the expression you had on your face was identical to one my niece makes. Shit, you guys could have been twins in that moment. Once I saw that, everything fell into place. Her eyes are the same as yours, and you guys even have the same dimple."

"You didn't say anything, Shawn. You didn't even let on a little bit," Jack said.

"Listen, man, I don't want to know what happened between you and my sister, and confronting you about it would come with a whole lot of explaining on your end. That's something I don't even want to mess with. It happened. It's a little fucked up, but it's in the past. Get me?"

"But you didn't bring it up to me either," I said.

Shawn shrugged. "If I guessed right, I knew you'd be confessing at some point. And, with you guys dating now, I figured you wouldn't be able to keep it a secret for long."

"I can't believe you guessed that Jack was the father," I said. "That feels so random."

He took a drink of his coffee. "It's not random at all. If you do the math, you had to have gotten pregnant sometime around the draft. Plus, when you got back from New York, you were a fucking disaster. I had a feeling something had happened; I just didn't know what." The look he gave to Jack made one thing extremely clear. Shawn wasn't happy that Jack had caused me to be that fucking disaster.

After quickly peeking at Jack, I saw that he'd gotten Shawn's point.

I couldn't even wrap my head around this.

"Shawn, I'm so sorry," I whispered.

"I know, and I get why you didn't tell me. Jack's my agent, and there's a lot riding on our professional relationship. We have contracts worth millions of dollars. In all honesty, it was probably best that you didn't tell me because I don't know what I would have done to him. But, now, I handle situations a little different-ly." His eyes scanned between Jack's and mine. "I don't know why you two hooked up and never spoke again until the Super

Bowl, and I don't want to know. Like I said before, that shit is in the past."

I put my hands on top of my head and glanced between both men. "I don't know what to say. I thought you'd be much more pissed about this. And the reason we're staying at a hotel is because I thought you'd be too angry for us to crash here."

"Getting angry and yelling isn't going to change what happened," he said. "You both fucked up, and you came clean. Now, we're moving on." He put his hand on top of mine, rubbing it over my fingers like he was trying to mess up my hair. "If it makes you feel any better, I've lied to you a few times, too."

"Yeah," I sighed. "But I can't imagine any of those instances could even compare to this one."

He laughed. "I'm sure I've got one that comes close."

"Please..."

"You want to go there, little sis? All right, how about this one? I used to sleep with Anna."

My mouth dropped open. "No."

"Oh, yeah. It went on for years. She used to sneak into my room in the middle of the night, and she'd return to yours early in the morning before you woke up."

I leaned back in my chair, my arms crossed over my chest. I knew Anna better than anyone. This almost felt like a challenge. "She would have told me."

"Wouldn't most people think you would have told me about Jack?"

He had me.

Regardless, I couldn't see them together. I couldn't even picture it in my head.

"We're still not even," I said. "But I'll admit, that was a good one."

Shawn looked at Jack after several seconds. "I'm warning you right now, you'd better be a good father to Lucy, and you'd better give those girls everything they need."

"You have my word," Jack said.

Shawn's eyes scanned back to me. "Lucy's getting a father, and that's all she's ever wanted. Don't fuck this up."

"I won't." I glanced at Jack. "I can't believe he's not strangling you for getting me pregnant at nineteen, and he's not kicking my ass out."

"Let's not keep reminding me of the nineteen-year-old detail, okay?" Shawn said.

I laughed.

God, it felt good.

Then, my brother replaced my glass with his mug. "Drink some coffee. You look like hell, and I imagine that's from not sleeping much last night. Once you guys bring your bags inside, we'll go out for brunch to put some food in your stomach. You two are staying here tonight, so call and cancel the goddamn hotel."

My eyes connected with Jack's again.

He'd told me not to worry.

Somehow, he'd known.

I didn't know how. I didn't care.

I just knew I was with two of my favorite guys, and nothing had changed between us.

33

SAMANTHA

Me: I survived.
Anna: Good, but how did it go?
Me: Much better than I thought. He sorta knew. He'd put it together when Jack went to see him in Nashville. I still don't know how. I guess he's smarter than all of us. LOL.
Anna: See? I told you it wasn't going to be that bad.
Me: I know. Jack did, too. I should have listened to you both.
Anna: Now, go enjoy the rest of the day with your brother, and stop stressing. Have fun.
Me: Oh, you mean, my brother...as in your EX?
Anna: He didn't.
Me: He did.
Anna: I can't believe that motherfucker threw me under the bus. He's going to get the wrath of me like he's never seen before.
Me: Be easy on him. Lucy needs her uncle, and Nashville really needs their starting tight end.
Anna: Girl, you're saying that to the wrong person. I model my feet for a living. I own the highest, sharpest, spikiest heels they make. Wait until he sees what I can do with my feet.

Me: I'm not sure if you're going to stab him or feet-fuck him. Either way, I don't want to know. I'm just bummed it didn't work out between you two. You're already family, but a sis-in-law would have been so incredible.

Anna: It's too early for sappy. Please fly safe tomorrow, and text me when you get home. AND fuck Jack on that private plane. Ugh, I can't stand that you'll get to check off that fantasy before me. The thought is making me stabby. I have to go.

Me: God, I love you.

34

JACK

"I REALLY COULD HAVE DONE ALL the cooking," Samantha said as she stood in front of me, glancing toward my kitchen. "I don't know why you insisted on bringing in a chef for the night."

I hadn't just hired a chef.

I'd hired Chef Fern, the best private chef in Miami. With her came two assistants and three servers. My kitchen looked like we were hosting a fucking gala.

I put my hands on her face, moving her head so that she looked at me. "If you cooked, then you'd be spending the whole night in front of the stove. I don't want that. I want you hanging out with our friends."

She released a long breath and wrapped her arms around my waist. "But this is costing you a fortune and—"

I cut her off with my lips, kissing the fuck out of hers.

It was cute as hell that she was worried about money. But she didn't have to. I'd just made five million off her brother, and he was only one of my clients.

Hiring a chef for the night certainly wasn't going to break me.

When I pulled my mouth back, I asked, "Is Lucy still in the shower?"

"Yes, and it was a huge mistake, letting her use your bathroom, because I'm not sure I'll ever be able to get her out. She can't stop squealing over the jets in the walls."

I laughed and brushed my lips across hers, needing a small taste again. "Let her have fun." I held her face tighter. "Maybe, if she loves my shower enough, she'll start nagging you about moving in here, and then she can shower in there every day."

Her stare softened. "Are you ready for us to move in, Jack?"

"Yes." I gripped her with so much more force. "Say the word, and I'll have the movers at your apartment tomorrow."

She took a breath. "Let's sleep on it, and we'll talk to Lucy about it tomorrow."

I pressed my nose against hers. "I can't wait to have the two of you living here with a wedding band on your finger and our second child growing in your belly." I drew back, so she could see my eyes. "But, this time, I'm going to be there when you deliver, and I'm going to watch my child come into this world."

"Mmm," she sighed, leaning her body into mine. "Everything you just said was so perfect, except for one teeny-tiny part."

"Which is?"

"When you said you were going to watch your child come into this world."

My brows rose. "You're going to stop me from doing that?"

"You see, you spend a significant amount of time between my legs. Some days, you lick me so much, I wonder how your tongue doesn't fall off. But I'm afraid that, once you see the baby crown, every fantasy you've ever had about my pussy will come to a screeching halt. So, you can hold my hand, and you can let me dig my nails into your skin, but you will stay above my waist. No exceptions."

Normally, bossiness like that would make me lift her into my arms, set her on the first surface I came to, and fuck those demands right out of her.

But this was an argument worth having later on when the time came because Samantha's pussy was one of the most beautiful things I'd ever seen. My child coming out of her wouldn't change my opinion. And, once she was cleared by her doctor, my tongue would be right back between her legs, doing one of the things I loved the most.

"Go finish getting ready, and I'll make us some drinks. Everyone should be here in twenty minutes."

She leaned into my lips, breathing against them for several seconds, before she turned around to head toward my bedroom.

I watched her walk, thinking about her goddamn ass and how she'd begged me to fuck it last night. When she disappeared behind the door, I shook my head and went to the bar, pouring myself several fingers' worth of scotch. I got Samantha a glass of wine, and I carried both into the kitchen.

"Are we all set?" I asked the staff.

The chef stopped mixing whatever was in the large bowl and said, "Sure are, Mr. Hunt. We're prepared to start passing appetizers as soon as your guests arrive. We'll also be setting up a station near your living room where they can help themselves to some shellfish on ice. We'll serve dinner about forty-five minutes later, followed by the sundae and cookie station you requested for your daughter."

My daughter.

I fucking loved hearing that.

And my daughter was going to freak out when she saw all the cookies and ice cream and frosting and candies I'd requested. Samantha was probably going to kill me for giving her that much sugar before bed. But I didn't care.

Tonight was important, and I wanted to spoil my kid.

I thanked the chef and her staff, and I moved toward my

bedroom, hearing Samantha and Lucy giggle as soon as I got to the door.

"Is everyone decent?" I called out.

"Jack!" Lucy yelled. "Come in."

I stepped inside and noticed they were in the bathroom, Lucy sitting on the counter while Samantha did her hair.

"What's so funny?" I said from the doorway.

"Lucy asked if she could have her birthday party in your bathroom."

"My bathroom?"

"Yes!" She moved her arms in front of her, her fingers shooting to the right and then the left, like her little hands were airplanes. "That's what your water is like, Jack. It's everywhere! My friends will *looove* it. So, can we? Can we have a party in there?"

This had to be a joke.

A bunch of eight-year-olds didn't want to hang out in my goddamn bathroom.

I needed to step this up a notch.

"How about we go to Disney instead?"

Lucy squealed, "Did you just say DISNEY?"

I gazed at Samantha. "We can take the plane to get all the kids there, rent a big suite for the night, and do a few of the parks. Then, we'll fly back the next day."

Samantha's eyes were so fucking large, I thought they were going to pop out of their sockets. After she gave me that look, she turned toward Lucy and said, "Baby, don't listen to your daddy. He's obviously lost his mind."

She didn't want me to spend the money.

I knew that was the cause of her reaction.

I moved over to them, putting an arm around Samantha's waist and another one around Lucy's shoulders. "Your dad hasn't lost his mind. I actually think it's one of the best ideas I've come up with."

"We'll talk about this later," Samantha said, wrapping the final twist around Lucy's ponytail.

"Mommy, Jack said Disney. He said he wants to bring me and my friends to Disney. Oh my God, DISNEY."

Samantha groaned and gave me the eye again. "I hope you realize you've just created a monster."

I laughed at both of their faces. Their expressions couldn't be more opposite. "Lucy, we'll discuss Disney tomorrow once your mom warms up to the idea a little."

I kissed Samantha's cheek and gave her the softest growl that I was sure Lucy couldn't hear. But I knew Samantha could, and she knew exactly what I meant by it. She was getting my tongue later tonight after Lucy went to bed in the room Samantha had decorated for her.

All of us were sitting in the living room after dinner and dessert—Max and Eve, Brett and James, Scarlett and Vince. My couch wasn't big enough to hold everyone, so James and Samantha took the floor, and Lucy was sitting on my lap.

This was the first night they had all met my daughter, and it had gone better than I'd planned. They'd spoiled the hell out of her, showing up with so many goddamn gifts. Samantha was overwhelmed by their generosity, especially with presents like a year's worth of horseback riding lessons and getting to have lunch with Taylor Swift.

She'd eventually get used to the way my friends and I spent money because I planned on dropping plenty of it on her and Lucy.

I wanted to give them everything, and I could afford to do it.

The four of us from The Agency had come from nothing. We'd grown up in rent-controlled apartments in Boston, and that was what had fueled us to get to where we were, what had driven us to keep fighting and never backing down. We didn't take our success for granted, and we appreciated every fucking second of it.

But my priorities had recently changed.

I wasn't just working for me anymore.

I was working for Samantha and my daughter.

I looked around the room, at everyone on the couch and on the floor. We were all a little sluggish after eating so much, and the room had turned quiet.

Max held up his phone and said, "Lucy, what's your favorite song? I'm going to play us some music."

I didn't know the answer to this one.

I wished I'd thought of asking it before Max.

"My favorite song is 'Lucy in the Sky with Diamonds,'" Lucy replied.

I turned her little body, so I could see her face. "That's your favorite song, too?"

I couldn't believe what she'd just said.

"Mommy told me she named me after that song because, when she was in the car with you, you were singing it." She talked loud enough for the whole room to hear, and she put her arm around my neck. "It's been my favorite ever since I was little, and now, I know it's your favorite, too."

The room was silent, and I could feel every set of eyes on me.

I looked at Samantha, trying to keep my emotions in check, but fuck, it was hard. "It was playing in the taxi that night," I said softly. "On our way back to the hotel."

She nodded, and I could tell she was struggling with her feelings as well. "You asked the taxi driver to turn up the radio. You sang every word to me, and then you told me how much you loved it."

"See, Jack? I told ya," Lucy said.

I kissed her on the cheek and glanced back at her mother.

We had an audience.

I didn't care.

"You named our daughter after my favorite song and Jacklyn as her middle name."

"I couldn't give her you, so I gave her every piece of you that I could."

I barely had time to take a fucking breath before the song began to play softly in the background.

Lucy wiggled off my lap, moving out from underneath my arm, and now, she was standing in front of me, tugging on my fingers. "Come dance with me, Jack."

I couldn't say no.

As Samantha wiped the corners of her eyes, I rose from the couch, and I let Lucy lead me to the middle of the living room. She stepped onto my feet, her sparkly shoes resting on my leather ones, and she tried so hard to reach my shoulders.

She wasn't even close.

I bent down and lifted her into the air until her hands were resting on me, my arm tightly holding her back.

"Much better," she said. "Now, we can really boogie."

I swayed our bodies and belted out the lyrics while Lucy sang along with me.

My daughter.

It was a word I'd gotten used to.

One I fucking loved to say.

"Lucy, hold on; I'm going to dip you," I told her when we got to the first chorus.

"Yay!" She giggled.

Her laughter was my favorite sound.

Right before I leaned Lucy toward the ground, I glanced at Samantha. Tears were dripping from her eyes, emotion filling her whole face, her hand pressing against her heart.

I fucking loved that woman.

Eight years had passed between us.

I didn't want another second to go by without her knowing how deep my love was.

While the most important people in my life watched me from the other side of the living room, I put my hand up to Lucy's ear, and I whispered several words.

When I finished, she turned her face toward me and said, "Really? I can say that?"

I nodded. "Yes, sweetheart, you can."

She looked at her mom, and with my encouragement, she said, "Mommy, Jack wants to know if you'll marry him."

EPILOGUE

LUCY

MOMMY HAD BOUGHT me pancake mix the last time she was at the store. I made her keep it a secret because I didn't want Jack to know. She even got a big bag of chocolate chips because Jack loved them in his pancakes, and I loved them in mine.

When Mommy met me in the kitchen, I took out the box and the chocolate chips from the pantry, and I mixed them all together. With Mommy watching, I stood on the stool I used when I helped her cook, and I flipped each one.

Once all three were done, Mommy got out a tray, and I put the plate on top with a cup of coffee and a bowl of grapes—those were Jack's favorite, too.

"Looks like you're all set to go, baby," she said.

I smiled. I was just so excited.

I took the tray off the counter and very carefully walked toward their room.

Mommy and I had moved into Jack's as soon as they got married. Their wedding day was the best day ever. Mommy said she had finally married her Prince Charming, and Jack said he'd married the girl of his dreams. I had gotten to be the flower girl, and I'd sprinkled little petals all over the sand before Mommy walked down the beach to meet Jack.

Now, Mommy and Jack shared the big room, and I had my own room down the hall where everything inside was Titans blue. I'd sent Uncle Shawn pictures, and he thought it was so cool. I couldn't wait for him to come see it, but he was so busy with football. I still saw plenty of him because we flew to all of his games.

Usually, when I got to their room, I would run as fast as I could toward their bed, jump on top, and bounce until they woke up. But, today, I had a big tray I had to carry, and I couldn't spill Jack's coffee.

I went over to where he was sleeping, and I got on my knees and set the tray on the floor. "Hey," I whispered, pushing on his arm to wake him.

His eyes opened, and he let out a yawn. "Good morning, baby."

I smiled real big again. "I made you something." I pointed down, so he could see what I meant.

"Pancakes?"

"Yep! Chocolate chip ones!"

"They look delicious."

"I made them. Mommy helped, too."

I lifted the tray and set it on the bed, and Jack scooched over, so there was plenty of room.

Today was such a special day. We weren't just going to have pancakes. Mommy said we were going to the marina where we were going out on the boat. I loved the boat, and I loved when Jack drove it fast.

"I have something to tell you," I said.

He sat up a little, so he could take a big bite. "What?"

"I've waited all my life to tell you this." My shoulders pushed up, and I stood tall on my knees. "Happy Father's Day, Daddy."

He put his fork down, and I saw all kinds of tears in his eyes. "Come here, baby."

I wrapped my arms around him and squeezed as hard as I could.

"Say it again," he whispered.

I closed my eyes. "Daddy."

"Out of all the endorsements I've ever gotten, you just gave me the best one."

ACKNOWLEDGMENTS

Jovana Shirley, you're a treasure, and I just love you. Your heart, your talent, your vision, your ability to find the pretty that lies beneath is unlike anything I've ever seen. Thank you for always squeezing me in, for being there whenever I need anything, and for making my books shine. XO.

Nina Grinstead, I don't even know where to begin. There are no words that could even come close to expressing how much gratitude I have for you. Every day, I'm thankful I have you in my life. You are one of the most incredible people I've ever met, and I'm so fortunate to have you as a publicist and as a dear friend. I wouldn't want to do this with anyone but you. Love you.

Judy Zweifel, once again, you rock my whole world. Thank you for being a part of this, for treating my words with so much love. I'm so grateful for you.

Kaitie Reister, I love you, girl, so hard. You're my biggest cheerleader and such a wonderful friend. Thank you for everything. XO.

Shannon, you're incredible. I can't thank you enough for all your hard work and for putting up with us and for every insane request we made. You gave this book the sexiest face.

Ricky, my sexyreads, you made me reach, as you always do, but this journey was so different for us. You wiped my tears, you gave me the words I needed, and you answered every text. I couldn't have done this without you. Love you.

Kimmi Street, my partner in crime, I couldn't have done this book without you. You're the hand I always need to hold and the shoulder I always want to lean on and the virtual tissue that's there whenever I need it. You're the most incredible friend, and I'm so lucky to have you as my person. Love you so much.

Crystal Radaker, you made me dig so deep for this book. You helped me find that bit of angst that I never knew was living inside me. You made me a better writer, a better listener, a better storyteller. I'm beyond grateful for you and our friendship. Love you so much.

Donna Cooksley Sanderson, thanks for all of your support. Love you, lady. XX.

Extra-special love goes to Stacey Jacovina, Jesse James, Kayti McGee, Carol Nevarez, Julie Vaden, Elizabeth Kelley, RC Boldt, Jennifer Porpora, Melissa Mann, Katie Amanatidis, my COPA ladies, and my group of Sarasota girls whom I love more than anything. I'm so grateful for all of you.

Mom and Dad, thanks for your unwavering belief in me and your constant encouragement. It means more than you'll ever know.

Brian, my words could never dent the amount of love you give me. Trust me when I say, I love you more.

My Midnighters, you are such a supportive, loving, motivating group. Thanks for being such an inspiration, for holding my hand when I need it, and for always begging for more words. I love you all.

To all the bloggers who read, review, share, post, tweet, Instagram—Thank you, thank you, thank you will never be enough. You do so much for our writing community, and we're so appreciative.

To my readers—I cherish each and every one of you. I'm so grateful for all the love you show my books, for taking the time to reach out to me, and for your passion and enthusiasm. I love, love, love you.

BONUS SCENE

Do you want to read Jack and Samantha's wedding night scene?
Then, turn the page!

BONUS SCENE OF ENDORSED

JACK - WEDDING NIGHT

I unlocked the door of the suite and held it open, turning toward my wife as she stepped closer to the entryway. I didn't want to carry her inside. I wanted to watch her walk, seeing the way her gorgeous body moved in that dress and how her ass, outlined in white lace, looked so fucking perfect.

When she was finally parallel to me, she put her hand on the side of my face. "God, my husband is so handsome."

I slid my mouth to the center of her palm and kissed it. "I want you naked. Right now."

"You're going to have to help me do that. All of the buttons are in the back, and there are *tons* of them."

"I'll use my teeth."

She laughed, rubbing her thumb over my lips. "If Lucy wants this dress one day, I don't want to have to explain to our daughter that her father ate off the buttons to my wedding gown."

"I'll get them repaired."

She held me tighter, her stare focused on my mouth. "Let's save the eating for my pussy."

"Fuck," I hissed.

I loved when she said that word, when it was my tongue that she craved because it was something I wanted to give her constantly.

"Get in there," I ordered.

I followed behind her as she went inside, and she stopped after only a few feet.

"Jack," she gasped.

My arms circled her waist, and my hands pressed into her navel, my face dipping into her neck. I closed my eyes and breathed her in.

Cinnamon.

It was the same scent I'd been inhaling since she joined me at the edge of the water where we exchanged our vows. That was over six hours ago, and the smell still hadn't faded from her skin.

Every time I wanted a whiff of it, I never had to reach far to get it.

That was because the wedding was small; the space we'd chosen was extremely intimate.

Out of all the places in the world, Samantha had picked Key West.

It was special to her.

It was where we'd taken our first vacation, the only time she'd ever left Lucy for more than a week.

I didn't care where we got married. I just wanted our friends and family there. I wanted our daughter to watch as I put a ring on her mother's finger. I wanted to hear Samantha say she was going to be mine forever.

And I got everything I wanted.

Samantha turned her head, nuzzling her cheek against my chest. "It's so beautiful in here."

There were candles on every surface. Rose petals were scattered all over the floor.

The hotel had made sure Samantha had the wedding of her dreams.

And they had made sure that, tonight, my fantasies would be fulfilled.

"I can be as loud as I want, and I don't have to worry about waking up Lucy," she added.

Our daughter had gone back to my parents' hotel room after the reception. She'd stay with them tonight, and tomorrow, we'd have breakfast with her before we left for our two-week honeymoon in Italy. Since my parents lived in Boston, Lucy would be with my in-laws while we were away.

"I'm going to do everything in my power to make sure you're screaming all night long."

She slid around and faced me. "You do that every time you touch me, Jack. I just try really hard to keep my screams under control."

"Mmm," I growled. "Tell me what it feels like."

I reached behind her and found the first button, pushing it through the small hole. I moved to the next one, the dress slowly loosening as I worked my way down.

"When I feel your tongue on me, a sensation comes through my body. It starts right here." She placed her hand on my stomach. "It feels like a shiver. My skin becomes extra-sensitive, and I lose all control. I can't think; I can't breathe. I just anticipate what's about to happen and the intensity in which it's going to grab me."

I'd reached the midway point on her back, my hands moving as fast as they fucking could. "Give me more."

She quivered as my thumb brushed across the strap of her bra, and her exhale came out as a moan. "Your hands, they consume my thoughts. They feel just as good as your tongue."

I was so fucking tempted to rip the rest of this dress off, but knowing Lucy might want it someday stopped me. So, I picked up my speed and quickly reached the top of her ass, shoving the rest of it past her hips until it was on the floor.

My gaze slowly shifted up her body—at the bright blue heels she had on and the white lace panties and the strapless bra of the same color and material.

"Jesus Christ," I hissed, taking a step back so that I could get a better look at her. "I can't believe I get to have you for the rest of my life."

That body.

Those tits.

That flat stomach that would one day swell with another baby.

That neck that I never grew tired of kissing.

Those lips that constantly told me she loved me.

"Get over here," I barked, wrapping my hands around her and lifting her into the air.

She squealed as I tightly held her, moving her through the large suite and into the bedroom where I gently set her on top of the bed.

Covering the white comforter was more rose petals. Hundreds of them. And they surrounded her like goddamn angel wings.

"Don't move," I told her while I worked the knot of my tie and dropped the jacket, each layer of clothing joining those two on the floor.

When only my boxer briefs were left, I knelt on the carpet in front of the bed and spread her legs apart, pulling her ass to the edge of the mattress.

"They're cold," she whispered.

"My hands?"

She shook her head, fisting the petals and dropping them on top of her. "The roses."

I grabbed one before it fell and pressed it against her leg, the circular patterns I traced getting closer and closer to her pussy. Just before I reached it, I moved to her other thigh.

"Oh my God," she groaned. "That feels so good."

"Lie back."

She hardly had her head on the blanket before I tore through the lace panties, shredding them until she was completely bare. Holding the petal between my lips, I dragged it up and down her clit, watching the goose bumps grow over her skin.

"*Ahhh.*"

I fucking loved when she made that sound.

I slipped a finger inside her, twisting it until I was buried to my furthest knuckle, and after I pulled out, I did it again, repeating the pattern. Her hips lifted each time. Her breathing increased, her toes grinding into my shoulders.

With the petal still in my mouth, I focused on the top of her clit, flicking it up and down, giving her the softest amount of friction.

"Jack..."

I added a second finger and a third, the three forming a triangle that filled her and fucked her with the speed she needed. Within a few seconds, she was writhing beneath me, her stomach shuddering, her nails digging into my head.

When she stilled, I left my boxer briefs on the floor, and I moved up her body. As my cock reached her entrance, I placed a hand on her face to hold it steady. Then, I took the flower out of my mouth and rubbed it across her chest.

"You knew I'd like the feel of that, didn't you?" she panted.

"I had an idea, and now, I plan to keep them stocked in our house."

She smiled. "Oh, I love the thought of that."

My lips gently fell against hers, and I teased the crown of my dick with her wetness. It felt so fucking good, so warm, so tight on my tip.

"My wife," I growled.

It was a word I still wasn't used to saying even though I'd considered her my wife from the second she accepted my proposal.

"My husband," she whispered back.

"Mmm. Say it again."

"Husband."

By the end of the first syllable, I was fully plunged inside her. I didn't hold back.

And I showed no mercy.

Because, as much as Samantha liked when I took my time, she liked my power even more.

Her head tilted into the mattress, and a scream came from the lips I'd just been kissing. "Jack, my God, don't stop."

I leaned up, gripping her thighs and lifting them, so her ass slapped against me.

She immediately began to tighten, and her screams got even louder. Her wetness dripped over my cock and leaked onto my balls. With each quiver of her stomach, her nails dug into me even harder.

Within a few pumps, my hips circling so that my dick stayed deep within her, my own orgasm was starting to work its way through.

She was on the edge, so I gave her several more twists of my hips, and I brushed a finger across her clit.

I knew that was all she needed.

And I was right because she screamed, "Jack, I'm coming!"

So was I.

As her pussy clenched, it milked the cum right out of me.

When we both finished, I dropped her thighs and collapsed on top of her, my arms holding all of my weight. "There are six dozen roses on this bed," I told her, "and every petal is going to touch your pussy tonight."

"What about all the ones in the other room?"

I gave her a quick kiss, and then I scooped her up and carried her into the bathroom, setting her on the edge of the tub. I turned on the water and watched it fill the bottom before I sprinkled flowers in there as well. "We're going to leave those right where they are. But there are lots more; don't you worry."

"More? Are you going to keep those as a surprise?"

I held her hand and helped her climb into the large tub. "You're going to get those tomorrow on the plane. I have a nine-hour flight to rub those petals over your skin."

Her brows rose. "We're flying private?"

I laughed and moved in behind her, my arms circling her waist. "Will you ever get used to this lifestyle, Samantha Hunt?"

She leaned her head against my chest and sighed. "It feels like a fairy tale."

That was because she was my princess, and nothing would ever change that.

MARNI'S MIDNIGHTERS

Getting to know my readers is one of my favorite parts about being an author. In Marni's Midnighters, my private Facebook group, we chat about steamy books, sexy and taboo toys, and sensual book boyfriends. Team members also qualify for exclusive giveaways and are the first to receive sneak peeks of the projects I'm currently working on. To join Marni's Midnighters, click HERE.

ABOUT THE AUTHOR

Best-selling author Marni Mann knew she was going to be a writer since middle school. While other girls her age were daydreaming about teenage pop stars, Marni was fantasizing about penning her first novel. She crafts sexy, titillating stories that weave together her love of darkness, mystery, passion, and human emotions. A New Englander at heart, she now lives in Sarasota, Florida, with her husband and their two dogs. When she's not nose deep in her laptop, working on her next novel, she's scouring for chocolate, sipping wine, traveling, or devouring fabulous books.

Want to get in touch? Visit me at...
www.marnismann.com
MarniMannBooks@gmail.com

ALSO BY MARNI MANN

STAND-ALONE NOVELS

Signed (Erotic Romance)

The Unblocked Collection (Erotic Romance)

Wild Aces (Erotic Romance)

Prisoned (Dark Erotic Thriller)

THE PRISONED SPIN-OFF DUET—Dark Erotic Thriller

Animal—Book One

Monster—Book Two

THE SHADOWS SERIES—Erotica

Seductive Shadows—Book One

Seductive Secrecy—Book Two

THE BAR HARBOR SERIES—New Adult

Pulled Beneath—Book One

Pulled Within—Book Two

The MEMOIR SERIES—Dark Fiction

Memoirs Aren't Fairytales—Book One

Scars from a Memoir—Book Two

SNEAK PEEK OF CONTRACTED

Turn the page to read the prologue of Contracted, *which is Max's story, that's releasing on June* 21.

PROLOGUE

MAX - TWO YEARS AGO

"GET UP," Brett said as he walked into his condo. He'd left me on the couch, watching the Heat game, to go to the lobby of his building and pick up the pizza he'd ordered. "We're going to James's."

As he went into the kitchen and grabbed a twelve-pack from the fridge, carrying it into the living room, I flipped off the TV. The look on my face told him exactly how I felt about the bullshit he'd just said to me.

"What?" he asked.

"Why the fuck are we going to James's?"

"I just saw her downstairs with her stylist, and they need my approval on some outfits."

James Ryne, Brett's newest client, had recently relocated to Miami and was renting a place in his building. America's sweetheart had escaped LA when a sex tape came out that ruined her whole career, taking her from one of the highest-paid actresses in Hollywood to unemployable. She'd hired our company, The Agency, to represent her, and Brett was now her agent.

Just because she worked with us didn't mean I wanted to spend my downtime with her. I hardly got any time off. My musicians were as high maintenance as Brett's actors. So, when I wasn't working, I wanted to relax and chill with my buddies.

Looking at some dresses wasn't that.

What it sounded like was fucking hell.

"And what am I?" I asked him, unsure of why he couldn't go to her place by himself. "A chaperone?"

"You're the fourth wheel."

I shook my head. "Not interested."

"Her stylist is hot as fuck. Trust me, brother."

Brett and I had the same taste in women. If he said she was hot as fuck, then I knew she must really be something to look at.

My feet slid off the cushion and dropped to the floor. "Now, I'm interested." I stood, taking the pizza boxes out of his hand, so he could carry the beer, and I followed him to the elevator. "It surprises me that you let the realtor move James into your building."

Jack and Scarlett, our other two business partners and best friends, also lived in downtown Miami high-rises. But not me. I didn't want to share walls or risk the chance of running into a client or an ex in the lobby. My fucking luck, I'd end up living above someone I'd dated, and I'd have to see her every goddamn morning at the gym.

That shit wasn't for me.

So, I'd bought a house on the water that was only a few minutes away. I didn't have a hell of a lot of land, but I had a direct view of Biscayne Bay that was prettier than any of those fuckers had.

"Why?" he asked.

"You won't even bring the women you fuck back to your place because you don't want them to know where you live, but you'll let James be a neighbor."

"It's different."

I laughed as we stepped into the elevator, Brett hitting the button for James's floor.

"What's so funny?"

He'd forgotten we'd practically been brothers since we were kids. All these years later, and I could still see right through him.

"Something tells me you didn't mind running into her."

"Jesus, don't start with me."

I continued laughing and shook my head. "I'm not starting shit. I'm just saying, if a girl who looked like James lived by me, I wouldn't exactly be pissed off about it. But you're not me, and going down to her apartment isn't you."

"She's my client."

"So, that makes this different? If anything, it should make it worse."

"It makes her off-limits," he snapped. "We're going to her place to see some dresses. That's it."

He was getting worked up, proving my point even further, and that only made me laugh harder.

"Something you could do in the office," I said.

"You're fucking starting again."

"And, now, I'm dropping it."

Brett moved, so I couldn't see his face. He'd done that on purpose, which was the final bit of proof I needed.

Damn it, I loved it when I was right.

Eventually, he'd admit it since he sucked at keeping secrets from me.

We stepped out of the elevator and walked down the hall. When we reached the apartment, Brett knocked on the door, but James wasn't the one who answered it.

Jesus fucking Christ.

The chick standing in front of us was the hottest woman I'd ever seen. And that wasn't something I said often, considering I worked in the music industry and was surrounded by the most beautiful women in the world.

Brett said hello to her, and then he immediately walked into the apartment.

I didn't.

I stayed right where I was, not wanting to move a goddamn inch unless it was to get closer to her. I lifted my hand off the bottom of the pizza boxes and held it out. "Max Graham," I said.

As she shook it, I felt the lightness of her grip, the softness of her skin, the heat that poured through her fingers.

"Eve Kennedy, James's stylist."

She was too gorgeous to be a stylist. She should act or model or stand naked in my office, so I could look at her every moment of the fucking day.

"Brett and I are partners," I told her in case she thought I was the pizza delivery boy.

"Do you represent actors like Brett?"

"Nah, I work with musicians."

Her brows rose, and I could tell she was intrigued. "Really? I need to hear more about this. I'm a music junkie."

"How about you invite me in first?"

"Oh my God, I'm so sorry. I didn't mean to keep you standing in the hallway with food. Come in, please."

Once I got inside, I set the pizzas on the table, and I grabbed a beer that Brett had put in the fridge.

"James will be right out," Eve said to him. "She wanted to take a quick shower before she tried anything on."

I held the pizza box open for Eve. After she took a slice, I got one for myself, and then the three of us went into the living room. Brett and I sat on the couch, and Eve took a spot on the ottoman.

"I spoke to your team and kept their recommendations in mind when choosing each dress," Eve said to Brett, now in full business mode. "Several are black, but more than half are in jewel tones, which look incredible with James's skin tone..."

I stopped listening.

I wasn't interested in their conversation.

Instead, my mind was picturing Eve in the shower with water dripping down her skin. Her long, lean legs spread just enough that I could see underneath her pussy, her C-sized tits having the hardest fucking nipples.

When I realized she had caught me staring at her, I wedged the beer between my knees and took a bite of my slice. "When does the fashion show start?"

"Right now," James said.

I looked in James's direction but only for a few seconds because my gaze was being dragged back to Eve. She was speaking to Brett about the dress James had on, and I was watching the way her lips moved. How her tongue casually licked the inside corner of her mouth. How her eyes had turned so serious.

I wondered what her expression would be if I told her where I wanted to put my tongue.

"So, what do you think?" Eve asked Brett.

"It's good," Brett said. "Let's see the next one."

Neither of the ladies knew Brett like I did, so they had no idea he was doing everything in his power not to toss James over his shoulder and carry her to the closest bed. But his face and his voice told me how hard he was fighting that urge.

I wasn't too far behind him.

This fashion show needed to end. I was more interested in spending time with Eve than watching James put on these fucking dresses.

"How many will she be trying on?" I asked.

"Twelve," Eve said.

That meant we had eleven more to go.

The only good thing about this situation was that Eve's attention would be on James, and that meant my attention could be on her.

And that was what I planned to do the whole time my ass was on this couch—memorize every inch of her, every twitch of her lips, every freckle I was able to see.

Finishing off my slice of pizza, I grabbed my beer, kicked my legs onto the ottoman not far from where Eve was sitting and said, "Looks like we're going to be here for a while, so I might as well get comfortable."

"Tell me some music dirt," Eve said, smiling at me, as the two of us stood on the balcony outside James's apartment. "I've only ever worked with actors. I'm so out of the know when it comes to your industry."

Once James had finished trying on all the outfits, I'd gone out to get some air, trying to calm my fucking cock. It had been hard since dress two. The smirk Eve had given me during dress eight had me gripping the goddamn armrest of the couch, so she wouldn't find herself tossed over my fucking shoulder and stripped naked on the way to a bedroom.

She shifted positions, looking at me from the corners of her eyes, and it sent me her smell. It reminded me of a New England summer night that had hints of orange and leaves.

Those were some of my favorite scents.

Fuck.

I glanced away for a second, and then I turned toward her again, catching the tail end of her grin. "What do you want to know?"

"Who doesn't write their own lyrics? Who lip-syncs? You know...the dirt."

Even her voice was sexy.

It was a little raspy, like she'd been screaming from all the things my tongue was doing to her cunt.

"You're asking the wrong person," I said.

"No, I think I'm asking the right one. Something tells me you just need a little incentive to spill."

I heard the door slide open, and Brett stuck his head through the opening. "I'm going to head up."

"I'll be there in a little while," I told him.

Once the glass was closed, my eyes went back to Eve's lips and the long piece of dark hair hanging down next to it. The strands were caught in her gloss, and it took everything I had not to move them. "What kind of incentive?"

The smile was back.

It was even larger now.

In the time I'd spent in this apartment, Eve had shown me she wasn't shy or timid at all. She was smart. Witty. And she had one hell of a mouth on her.

Before she could respond to my question, she needed to know something about me.

"I'm a forward kind of guy. I say what I want, and I rarely use a filter. In other words, I don't fuck around. So, just be straight up with me."

"I don't fuck around either."

Finally, it sounded like I'd met my match.

"Tell me what's on your mind," she continued.

I gently gripped her waist. If I pulled her any closer, she'd be able to feel my cock, so I kept her a few inches away, but I leaned into her ear, so I could whisper what was on my mind.

I knew she wanted the same thing because her body tightened.

Her neck tilted back, giving me more skin to breathe against.

She sighed into the hot Miami air.

Before this night was over, this body was going to be mine.